The buffalo hunter took the dead Indian's knife, slipped it under his belt, and stepped over to the pinto. Standing on the far side of the animal, he checked the bridle and was about to turn and reach for his rifle when he abruptly started, gasping. Standing halfway down the slope, holding his own rifle at waist level with both hands, was the formidable figure of Marshal Will Hardin. The ominous black muzzle of the repeater rifle was pointing straight at the killer's broad chest, just over the top of the pinto's back.

Cougar's harsh voice cut the air like a bullwhip. "Don't bother going for your weapon, Silcox! Raise your hands and step around the horse!"

Instead of complying, a broad grin worked its way across the ugly man's bearded face. Meeting Cougar's icy gray glare, he laughed malevolently and retorted, "Reckon it had to come to this, didn't it? We finally get our showdown after a long chase."

The Badge Series
Ask your bookseller for the books you have missed

Book 1: SUNDANCE
Book 2: THE FACELESS MAN
Book 3: THE BLACK COFFIN
Book 4: POWDER RIVER
Book 5: LONDON'S REVENGE
Book 6: THE SHOWDOWN
Book 7: THE IMPOSTOR
Book 8: THE STRANGER
Book 9: BACKLASH
Book 10: BLOOD TRAIL
Book 11: DARK CANYON
Book 12: DEATH LIST
Book 13: THE OUTCAST
Book 14: THE GALLOWS
Book 15: FARRELL'S WAR
Book 16: CANNON'S GRAVE
Book 17: THE VULTURE
Book 18: COUGAR

THE BADGE: BOOK 18

★

COUGAR

★

Bill Reno

 Created by the producers of
**The Holts: An American Dynasty,
Stagecoach,** and **White Indian.**

Book Creations Inc., Canaan, NY • Lyle Kenyon Engel, Founder

BANTAM BOOKS
NEW YORK • TORONTO • LONDON • SYDNEY • AUCKLAND

COUGAR

*A Bantam Book / published by arrangement with
Book Creations, Inc.*

Bantam edition / August 1990

*Produced by Book Creations, Inc.
Lyle Kenyon Engel: Founder*

ISBN 0-553-28567-X

Published simultaneously in the United States and Canada

*Bantam Books are published by Bantam Books, a division of Bantam
Doubleday Dell Publishing Group, Inc. Its trademark, consisting of
the words "Bantam Books" and the portrayal of a rooster, is
Registered in U.S. Patent and Trademark Office and in other
countries. Marca Registrada. Bantam Books, 666 Fifth Avenue,
New York, New York 10103.*

PRINTED IN THE UNITED STATES OF AMERICA

RAD   0 9 8 7 6 5 4 3 2 1

COUGAR

James Bowie died in 1836 while defending the Alamo, but about five years earlier he invented a style of knife that would forever bear his name. While bowie knives vary considerably, a few characteristics are common to most: a wide, strong, single-edged blade from six to eighteen inches long that tapers to a double-edged point; a false edge that protrudes on each side of the blade; and a symmetrical guard on the handle. The knife was good for hunting and fishing, but perhaps it is best remembered for its efficacy in a fight.

Chapter One

The Bighorn Mountains to the west were still snow-capped and a bite was in the air as the stagecoach rolled to a halt in front of the stage office at Sheridan, Wyoming, on the last day of March 1883. Newlyweds Lanny and Marie Caldwell alighted from the coach, and the young woman looked around expectantly. Pointing up the deeply rutted street, she exclaimed, "Here they come!"

The older couple in the approaching wagon waved, then Hec Stebbins braked his buckboard to a stop. Hopping down, he then helped his wife from the wagon, and the Stebbinses embraced first their daughter, then the son-in-law they had never met.

Hec asked the young couple, "Well, what do you think of Sheridan? It's grown some since you left for Kansas City two years ago, eh, Marie?"

Looking around and smiling, Marie agreed that the settlement had indeed grown. The town now boasted a dry goods store, an eating establishment, a general store, a saddlery shop, a doctor's office and pharmacy, and three saloons. What pleased her most, she remarked, was the new boardwalk, which ran the full four-block length of Main Street.

At that moment a stalwart-looking man with a Colt .45 slung low on his right hip and a badge pinned to his shirt emerged from the marshal's office directly across the street. Seeing the lawman, Hec Stebbins motioned him over, then said to Marie and Lanny, "Somethin' else, too. We've got us a town marshal now." As Zack Traynor ambled across the street, Hec gave the young couple an ironic smile, observing, "Unfortunately, good folks aren't the only ones attracted to growth and progress. We've got our share of drifters—buffalo hunters comin' to town for drinkin' binges, and the occasional outlaw ridin' through. But Zack's more'n able to handle 'em."

Marshal Zack Traynor had just turned fifty, but he looked a good five years younger. Of medium build and average height, Traynor's hair and thick walrus mustache were still dark and barely showing gray. Beneath a broad-brimmed hat, he wore a lightweight jacket, flannel shirt, and trousers and seemed oblivious to the chill. As he made his way across the street, the highly polished badge pinned to his plaid shirt glinted in the sunlight.

Hec Stebbins introduced Traynor to his daughter and son-in-law. Welcoming them home, the lawman told Lanny, "Your father-in-law said you'll be building a new house on your property. I'm right glad to hear it. It's good to have family around in case of trouble."

"Yes, sir," Caldwell agreed.

Zack Traynor's attention was suddenly drawn to the north end of Main Street. Amid the buggy, wagon, horse, and pedestrian traffic, six hard-faced riders were coming directly toward him. Stiffening, he said softly, "Speaking of trouble, here it comes now."

Hec Stebbins pivoted to see what the marshal was talking about. Responding softly, the rancher remarked, "Just the appearance of that bunch is enough to convince me that I'm looking at troublemakers."

Traynor gazed up and down the street at the many people milling about. "Hec," he ordered quickly, "do what you can to clear the street. There's liable to be gunplay."

"You know those dudes?"

"Yeah. They were here last week. One of their pals got liquored up and decided to use me for target practice. I had to kill him. His cohorts apparently realized they were too drunk to take me on, but they said they'd be back. I was hoping when they sobered up, they'd just move on and forget it—but obviously they didn't."

Hec Stebbins urgently told his son-in-law, "Lanny, get the women inside the stage office."

Caldwell nodded and ushered his wife and mother-in-law toward the office door. When Marie was slow to move, looking back over her shoulder at the oncoming riders, her husband took her arm and urged, "Hurry!"

Stepping off the boardwalk, Traynor walked into the street while loosening the Colt .45 in his low-slung holster. He had been a lawman in the West for nearly thirty years, but if words alone could not keep these scabrous-looking men from drawing their guns, Marshal Zack Traynor had seen his last sunrise. He was facing impossible odds, for there was no way one man could take out six opponents—especially when he only had five cartridges in his gun.

Sheridan's marshal was a careful man. The hammer of his revolver rested on an empty chamber, which to him was the only safe way to carry a gun. He had known of too many careless men who had shot their own leg having a live cartridge beneath the hammer. As the mean-eyed riders drew ever closer, he was reluctant to pull his weapon and be the aggressor, on the slim chance that he could talk the men out of their obvious intent.

Traynor watched the gang approach, peripherally aware that Hec Stebbins was dashing toward a cluster of men who stood in front of the Bighorn Saloon. Over the pounding of his heart, the lawman heard the rancher tell the group what was about to happen, asking them to help him get people off the street. However, many of the bystanders, curious as to how the confrontation would turn out, merely craned their necks to see the oncoming riders.

Marshal Zack Traynor's guts went as taut as fiddle strings as the riders drew up, then dismounted. They all had devilry in their eyes as they formed a half circle around the lawman.

Every group of hardcases the lawman had ever encountered had a leader, and this gang was no exception. This particular leader was a big, red-faced man with an unkempt orange-colored beard and mustache. His hat covered his head, but a scraggly fringe protruded above his large ears.

Tight-lipped, Traynor intently and coldly regarded all six men, then settled his gaze on the leader and warned, "I told you not to come back, Whitcomb."

"And I told you we *were* comin' back, Traynor!" Vince Whitcomb retorted. "You murdered Harry Newton, and we're here to even things up."

Traynor spoke slowly, and the muscles in his neck and shoulders ached from being taut. "I didn't murder your buddy, and you know it. You were drunk, but not *that* drunk. You know full well I did everything I could to keep him from trying to use his gun on me. When he aimed it at me, I had no choice but to take him out." The marshal paused briefly, then holding his voice level, added, "I advise you and your men to get back on your horses and ride on. Look around. There are at least fifty people watching you right now—and they'll all be eyewitnesses who will testify against you when the law runs you down and you go to trial."

The heavyset man standing next to Whitcomb chuckled wickedly and quipped, "Well, at least you're smart enough to know you won't be comin' out of this situation alive, Marshal."

Traynor's eyes glinted angrily as he replied, "Maybe I won't, but you can bet I'll get a couple of you before I die."

"We're bettin' you don't," the motley-looking man countered. "We're bettin' we can drop you cold before you can even pull your iron."

Suddenly a sharp voice sliced through the early-afternoon air, warning, "Touch your guns, scum, and you'll lose the bet!"

The rude jolt of surprise drew the attention of all the gang members. The men's heads whipped around toward the voice, and they focused on the intruder with hate-filled eyes. From the space between the stage office and the doctor's office, a tall, slender figure dressed in a fringed buckskin shirt and denim pants materialized. He was holding a Winchester .44 repeater firmly in his right hand, the muzzle angled toward the ground.

As the sinewy man stepped from the alleyway, everyone saw who had issued the challenge. Although his tan, wide-brimmed hat somewhat shaded his handsome, angular face, with its tawny mustache, it did not hide his glaring gunmetal-gray eyes or the four curved scars that swept across his left cheek from temple to mouth.

His name quickly passed along the street: *"Cougar!"*

The name reverberating along the street brought Marie Caldwell to the window of the stage office. One look and Marie said to her mother, "It's Will Hardin!"

The stage agent, a short, fat man, nodded and declared, "Now those birds will find out what it's like to run head-on into a buzz saw!"

"Who's this Cougar?" queried Lanny.

"Lightning on two legs," answered the agent. "See that rifle he's got?"

"Yes."

"He's got it rigged so when he works the lever, it bypasses the trigger. He can fire seven shots faster than you can blink twice." Gesturing with his chin, the agent added, "And you see that sheath on his belt? It's holding a knife with a ten-inch steel blade. The handle has a silver stud the size of a nickel that's stamped with his mark—a cougar paw with the claws distended. That young man— he's only twenty-three—forges them himself."

Cougar was cool and collected as he drew within thirty feet of the men who stood arrayed in front of Marshal Zack Traynor. Whenever his pale gray eyes settled on a man, they seemed to bore right through him, and at that moment, they settled on Vince Whitcomb, who stood poised and clearly ready to go for the gun on his hip.

Speaking in a voice of quiet authority, Cougar stated, "Get on your horses and ride, like the marshal said . . . unless you choose to die where you stand."

Whitcomb smiled humorlessly and ran a disdainful gaze up and down Hardin's long, wiry form, finally saying caustically, "You must not be able to count very good, mister. I don't see anybody else lookin' interested in joinin' you and the marshal—meanin' the odds don't look too good for your side." His eyes glinted, anticipating a battle.

Whitcomb's men stood waiting and watching for their leader to make his move. It came quickly. The burly man clawed for his gun, obviously figuring to kill the intruder while his friends took out the marshal. But Will Hardin's rifle came alive before Whitcomb's gun was even free of its holster, and two .44 slugs tore into the drifter's chest, killing him instantly. The impact of the two bullets coming within a split second knocked Whitcomb backward, and his lifeless form sprawled faceup, shock frozen on his ugly face.

Zack Traynor's hand reached for his revolver at the same instant Cougar cut loose, while the other drifters went for their weapons as their leader was blasted into eternity. Traynor shot one of the men through the heart and put a bullet in another's chest while Cougar's rapid fire put five slugs into the other three, killing them all before any of them could get off a shot. The gunfight was all over almost before it began.

The townspeople were mesmerized by the scene, and no one on the street moved. As the soft breeze carried the clouds of blue-white gun smoke away, Hardin stepped close to the marshal and said calmly, "You all right, Zack?"

"Yeah." Traynor nodded slowly and replied, "Thanks to you."

Small wisps of smoke were trailing from the muzzle of Cougar's rifle as he gazed at the bodies grotesquely sprawled and crumpled in the street. He started to say something when, from behind Traynor, he noticed the man the marshal had shot in the chest suddenly move. Lying on his back, the wounded man was bringing a derringer out from under his belt.

Cougar dropped his empty rifle and his hand flashed to the big knife at his waist. Before the marshal was aware of what was happening, the young man leapt past Traynor and threw the knife at the would-be assassin.

The drifter let out a strangled gagging sound as the knife buried itself in his throat. His body twitched as he dropped the derringer and desperately clutched the handle of the knife, then died with his fingers limply gripping it.

Zack Traynor wiped a shaky palm across his sweat-beaded brow. "Whew!" he gasped. "I must be slipping in my old age. I'd have sworn I killed that dude."

Hardin strode over to the dead man and yanked the knife from his throat. While using the drifter's shirt to wipe the blood from the blade, Cougar remarked over his shoulder, "It's not old age, my friend. You were just a little off balance because you were outnumbered." Straightening up to his full height, the lanky young man placed the knife back in its sheath and added, "You've been needing a deputy for some time now, Zack, and maybe you should finally do something about it. Too many ruffians are coming through Sheridan nowadays. You need somebody to watch your back."

The bystanders suddenly came alive again, gathering close to the gruesome scene and calling out their appreciation to Cougar for stepping in to help the marshal. Ralph Coe, the chairman of the Sheridan town council, stepped between the two men and laid a hand on Traynor's shoulder. Looking up with admiration at Hardin, the portly businessman declared, "I heard what you said, and I agree with you, Will. This bloody shoot-out right here is evidence enough that Sheridan needs a deputy . . . and I've got a particular man in mind."

"Good," Cougar responded. "Better get him here as quickly as you can."

"Don't have to send for him," Coe said evenly, a smile on his moon-shaped face. "I'm *looking* at him."

The crowd chorused their approval, and the marshal was enthusiastic as well. But shaking his head, Hardin began to back off, saying, "That wouldn't be possible. I've got too many irons in the fire—literally." Putting his hand on the sheath on his belt, he went on, "After all, forging these knives takes time—I've built up a reputation now, and I'm proud to say that people all over the West hanker after my stock." He stopped and grinned, then continued, "I guess it isn't tooting your own horn to repeat what lots of folks say—which is that mine are some of the most beautiful and well-balanced hunting knives they've ever seen. And to tell you the truth, I like getting both the recognition and the income."

Nodding, Ralph Coe remarked, "I can certainly understand your feelings, Will."

"And don't forget," Cougar added, "I also spend a fair amount of time tracking down predators for a living—both human ones that the government is after and big cats that take out ranchers' stock. The ranchers in particular rely on my help."

Ralph Coe looked thoughtful for a long moment, then finally stated, "Will, I realize the salary we can offer you probably wouldn't match what you make doing the tracking of outlaws, lions, and wolves, but . . . well, just to put it plain, we need you. Zack needs you. If you hadn't been in town today, this first-class lawman would be dead right now. Some of our citizens might have been killed, too. How about it? Won't you make all of us happy and say you'll take the job?"

Zack Traynor put his hand on Hardin's shoulder. "Will, the load in this town is getting too heavy for me to bear alone—and frankly there's not a man on earth I'd rather have at my side than you . . . even if you had to be gone at times. What would you say about taking the job if we were to have an agreement that when the ranchers need you to hunt down four-legged predators, you go and do it.

As for dealing with the two-legged kind, well, you'll certainly get your fill right here."

Cougar grinned. "You're no doubt right about that, Zack. Tell you what. I'll accept the job as long as I can be free to help out the ranchers and be able to keep making my knives to bolster my income. But if I'm going to be your deputy, that'll mean moving into town, so I'll need two things: a cabin to live in, and a blacksmith shop for my forge."

A sudden babel of voices erupted from the crowd, with citizens promising to provide the materials and the labor to construct both buildings.

Laughing, Cougar Will Hardin shook Zack Traynor's hand and agreed, "Okay, it's a deal. And to show you how much I believe in the job, I'll even forge my own badge."

Over the cheers of the onlookers, Traynor clapped his new deputy marshal on the back and told him earnestly, "Thank you, my friend, for saving my life today." Gesturing with his chin at the bodies of the troublemakers being carted away, the lawman added, "If you hadn't stepped in, they'd be carrying *my* body away."

Shaking his head slowly, Hardin replied wryly, "I couldn't let that happen. If you had been killed, the townsfolk would have wanted to make me *marshal* . . . and that's one job I *don't* want!"

As the lanky young man rode through the Bighorn Mountains toward his home, he thought how becoming deputy of Sheridan was a major turning point in his life. Then he touched the scars on his face and thought back eight years to another turning point, when he had been fifteen and encountered the mountain lion that had so indelibly etched him—literally and spiritually.

A big male cougar had crept onto his parents' place one night, stalking their milk cow. Young Will Hardin's small dog had begun barking at the huge cat, waking up his master. The teenager had raced out of the house, but by the time he reached the corral, the dog was dead.

Moonlight glinted off the youth's rifle, washing the rugged land with a silvery glow as he chased the cougar farther into the high country. Showing his mastery of reading signs as he made his way through the mountainous terrain, young Will Hardin was relentless in his pursuit. His eyes alternately scoured the ground and kept watch on the distant landscape as the night wore on and the search continued.

Finally, about two hours before dawn, he knelt to examine some freshly made tracks. Suddenly he heard a loud hiss behind him—a warning of death—followed by a wild roar. Quickly standing, he whirled around just as the cougar leapt at him from a high rock. The youth swung the muzzle of his rifle upward as the huge cat came swooping down at him like an enormous bird of prey. Hardin fired the weapon, putting a bullet in the cougar's heart, but not before the animal's sharp, vicious claws tore at the boy's face, raking the length of his left cheek.

After catching his breath and making sure the animal was dead, the boy—his face a bloody mess—hoisted the huge carcass over his muscular shoulders and started for home. As soon as he stepped through the door of the Hardins' cabin, Obadiah Hardin, a big, husky, rough and rugged mountain man, dubbed his son "Cougar," and the nickname stuck. The mountain lion's head was stuffed and hung prominently on the wall above the fireplace.

After the gashes had healed, the youth's stepmother, a Blackfoot Indian named Meadowlark, assured the handsome young man that his looks were actually enhanced by the scars. At the time, Will Hardin had some trouble believing her, but through the years the attentions of various young ladies in and around Sheridan had amply proved Meadowlark's pronouncement true.

Tall and strong as a youth, Cougar Will Hardin had grown to be over six feet tall, and he was as physically powerful and catlike in his movements as the animal for which he was nicknamed. He also had a fearsome reputation as a fighter, and while he never provoked a fight, neither did he shun one.

As he guided his horse carefully along the mountain trail, thinking about his past, Cougar wondered, as he often did, what his mother—his natural mother—had been like. She had died in childbirth, and his father had remarried about a year later. Hardin could not imagine a better mother than the one who had replaced his natural one, for Meadowlark, a beautiful and kind woman, loved him as though he were her own.

Quite well educated, she had been schooled by Methodist missionaries as a child and had passed on her love of learning to her stepson. Meadowlark's father, Red Wolf, had lived with them as long as Cougar could remember, and both his father and his adoptive grandfather had taught him at an early age how to track and hunt. Smiling to himself, the young man recollected that Red Wolf had declared not long ago that the student had surpassed both his teachers in hunting and tracking abilities and now put their considerable skills to shame.

Pressing his boots gently to his mount's sides, anxious to get home, Cougar Will Hardin said aloud, "I hope you're right, Grandpa. I have the feeling that as the new deputy marshal of Sheridan, Wyoming, those skills will be called on mighty often."

Chapter Two

By the first week of May, Will Hardin's small house and blacksmith shop had been built, and he was ready to move into town. On the last evening that Cougar would spend in his parents' mountain home, Meadowlark Hardin had arranged a farewell dinner, inviting their neighbors, Dale and Letha Simmons and their daughter, Veronica. Waiting for her guests to arrive, Meadowlark bustled around the Hardin cabin—a low-roofed building with three bedrooms and a large great room that served as both kitchen and living room—a smile of complicity on her beautiful face.

Always keenly interested in education, Meadowlark had grown very close to Veronica Simmons, who was Sheridan's schoolteacher. Now it was the Indian woman's deep desire to have the bright and beautiful twenty-one-year-old for her daughter-in-law, and though she had not pushed her stepson into a love relationship with Veronica, she did all she could to encourage it. Veronica, however, needed no prompting, and she had often visited Meadowlark, confiding of her love for young Hardin. While Meadowlark knew that Cougar deeply admired Veronica and cherished her friendship, affectionately calling her Ronnie, she also knew that he was so wrapped up in his work that he had never allowed a romance to develop. She dearly wanted his affection to turn to love . . . the marrying kind of love.

True to her mission to promote things between Cougar and Veronica, Meadowlark had invited Dale and Letha Simmons and their daughter to the special dinner. The sun was beginning to set when the Simmonses' wagon rolled into the yard, and Meadowlark heard the rancher, who owned a large and thriving spread a few miles south of Sheridan, call out a greeting.

The Indian woman stepped onto the porch and into the soft breeze that was blowing, filling the air with the scent of pine. A gleam of white caught the corner of her eye, and she glanced to her right where the lowering sun had touched a snowcapped peak in the distance, making it glisten like gold.

Cougar Will Hardin and the other two men in the family were sitting on the porch as their neighbors' buckboard hauled to a stop. Dale Simmons, a man of medium build and prematurely gray hair, helped Letha down from the seat, while Will Hardin hurried to assist Veronica, who, with her blond hair, blue eyes, and delicate figure, looked so much like her mother.

Smiling at her guests, Meadowlark wiped her hands on the apron that covered her long doeskin skirt and beaded blouse. Though married for more than two decades to a white man, she had retained her Indian ways—as well as her natural beauty. Barely into her forties, she was still quite youthful in appearance, and her small-boned frame was slender while her hair was still jet black.

"Welcome, my friends!" she exclaimed. "Dinner is just about ready. Come in and gather around the table."

Obadiah Hardin stood next to Red Wolf as Cougar and the guests filed through the door behind Meadowlark. Obadiah, a large man standing well over six feet and weighing nearly two hundred and forty pounds, was a true mountain man who wore his hair shaggy and sported a full beard. At forty-five, he was beginning to develop a paunch at his middle, though he was still as strong as an ox and as tough as nails. However, under his crusty façade was a gentle soul and a man of compassion.

Red Wolf, a small, bony man with dark and deeply wrinkled skin, was dwarfed by his white son-in-law. The old man had a thin, humped nose and prominent cheekbones, and like his daughter he wore Indian garb, including a bear-tooth necklace. His long, gray hair lay on his back in a braid, and a red bandanna, folded into an inch-wide strip, encircled his head.

Meadowlark directed the guests where to sit at the long table, purposely placing her stepson and Veronica across from each other, and she noticed the young woman stealing loving glances at Cougar. Many young men in Sheridan had tried to court Veronica, but she found one way or another to diplomatically refuse them, for her heart had belonged to Will Hardin since the day they had met four years earlier when Cougar had been nineteen and Veronica seventeen.

For the beautiful blonde it had been love at first sight, and from that day on she had had eyes only for the handsome Will Hardin. Her eyes were on him now, and the look in them and the expression on her face made it more than apparent to everyone but him how she felt—and how much she longed for him to love her in return.

During the meal Obadiah began reminiscing about his son's childhood, and it was readily apparent that Obadiah had difficulty accepting Cougar's leaving home. When Obadiah's reminiscence turned to the incident that had scarred his boy for life, all eyes automatically glanced at the stuffed head of the big cat over the fireplace. Obadiah had done the taxidermy, fixing the animal with wild-looking eyes and bared fangs.

After taking a sip of his coffee, Obadiah finished the story, explaining, "A lot of folks who know about Will and that big cougar don't know that neighboring ranchers and I had tried to track the beast several times but never could corner him." He looked at his son proudly. "Then this tousle-haired, fifteen-year-old kid set out to run him down and did it. At night, too."

Red Wolf let a slight grin curve his solemn mouth and announced, "You and I trained him well, Obadiah."

Meadowlark shook her head. "I do not think it was so much his training, Father, as it was his determination. Will wanted to kill that cat for taking the life of his little dog, Ruff."

Will Hardin glanced at the cougar head on the wall, then said, "You're right, Mother. Ruff was my best friend, and nothing on earth was going to keep me from getting revenge for his death."

"Well, you got your revenge, son," agreed Obadiah. "But you got something you didn't plan on when you killed that big cat: a new name for yourself."

"Yeah," Cougar admitted, grinning, "thanks to you." His hand went to the scars on the left side of his face. "I was one lucky kid. Those claws could just as easily have gouged my eyes as my cheek."

Meadowlark, who sat next to her stepson, patted his forearm and chided him, "You should never have set out on your own after that animal, especially in the middle of the night."

The young man grinned at Meadowlark and quipped, "You sound just like a mother."

Looking into his eyes, the Indian woman replied softly, "I didn't bring you into the world, son, but I couldn't love you any more if I had."

Will Hardin put his arm around her and hugged her tightly. "As far as I'm concerned, you are my mother." They looked into each other's eyes for a long moment, wordlessly sharing the bond between them. Then, lightening the moment, Cougar asked in a teasing voice, "What will I do without you at my elbow to keep me in line?"

Meadowlark wanted to suggest that Veronica could do a fine job in her place, but she held her tongue.

Dale Simmons then changed the subject, querying, "Will,

are you going to enter the knife-throwing and target-shooting contest this year?"

"Sure thing, Mr. Simmons. I wouldn't miss it for the world."

Veronica laughed and said, "With you in the contest, Will, it always means the best any of the other contestants can hope for is second place."

"I think it's been good for the other men who enter the contest that Will has taken first place in all three events for the past three years," put in Obadiah. "They all have to work extra hard to improve their skills."

"And I have to work extra hard to stay ahead of them," Will said with a laugh.

Meadowlark got up and began clearing the table, politely refusing Letha Simmons's offer of help. After handing her plate to her hostess, Letha then asked the guest of honor, "Will, I understand that you decided to make your own badge. Have you done so yet?"

"Yes, ma'am. It was the last thing I did before dismantling my equipment to move the shop into town." While the young man spoke, he unbuttoned the pocket of his fringed buckskin shirt, then produced the shiny new six-pointed star. Of steel and highly polished, it had the words DEPUTY MARSHAL engraved on its center.

Everyone wanted to see it, and the badge was passed around the table. The last person to take it was Veronica, and she held it in her hand, looking at it admiringly for a long moment, then reached across the table and returned it to Cougar. "I'm very proud of you, Will," she told him warmly.

As she handed it over to him, their fingers touched for a moment, and Veronica did not move her hand. When the new deputy slowly pulled his hand away and dropped the badge back in his pocket, the schoolteacher said, "I have a request of you, Will."

"Just name it," he responded.

"On the morning of the contest, will you come by the schoolhouse and give a knife-throwing demonstration for the children? It will be the last day of school before summer vacation, and my students would find it an exciting way to end the school year."

"Of course," Cougar promised.

"Good! Besides, I want the boys and girls to know what diligent practice can achieve."

At eight o'clock the next morning, Cougar Will Hardin arrived in town and moved the last of his belongings into his new house. That done, with the big knife strapped on his waist and carrying the specially rigged Winchester, he walked to the marshal's office, where Zack Traynor and the town councilmen were waiting for him.

Standing behind his desk as Cougar came through the door, the marshal smiled and said, "Well, Mr. Hardin, are you ready to become *Deputy* Hardin?"

"You bet," the lanky young man replied with a grin, his gaze taking in the faces of Ralph Coe and the other members of the council.

Will Hardin was sworn in, with Marshal Zack Traynor pinning the new badge on his deputy's chest. After the councilmen had left, the new lawman asked Traynor, "Okay, boss, what's first?"

"School," came the level reply.

Bewildered, Cougar echoed, "School?"

"Yep. You'll find that, as a lawman, carrying your rifle will be somewhat cumbersome. We all know that you're a deadeye when firing that repeater at a target, but now you're going to need to become skilled with a revolver at the fast-draw." He grinned wryly, adding, "And I've got a feeling you'll become skilled at it in no time."

He walked back to his desk and reached inside the bottom drawer. Pulling out a gun belt and holster, which held a shiny new Colt .45 with a pearl handle, he handed it to his new deputy. "Here. Consider this my way of thanking you for saving my life."

His eyes gleaming, Will Hardin took the gun belt and

strapped it on, thonging the holster to his thigh. "How about ammunition?" he asked.

The marshal shook his head. "First we'll try it empty. Come on. Let's go out back." The marshal then led the way into the alley behind the jail.

"Okay," said Traynor, "the first thing we have to do is find the right spot for your holster. It's important to have the gun at a level that's comfortable for you to draw without feeling that you're reaching for it. Most men like the butt to be even with the wrist. Others like it a little lower, and some like it higher."

Cougar let his right arm swing loose and found that the tip of the gun butt was exactly even with his wrist. The marshal told him to make a few draws with it there, then raise it and lower it, trying additional draws at the various levels. When he had found the spot that seemed the most natural, the deputy drew the empty gun repeatedly until he got the feel of it.

Watching the lithe young man, Traynor observed, "Just as I thought, Will. You're a natural. I'd say you're already drawing faster than the average man will ever do it."

Pausing to rest his arm, Cougar grinned proudly. "Really?"

"Really. Now, let me show you a couple of things that will improve your draw." The experienced lawman gave his student a few tips on stance, balance, and arm placement, all of which Hardin immediately incorporated into his practice. The marshal watched Cougar Will Hardin take to the fast-draw like an eagle takes to flight, then suggested they ride out of town to a tree-lined ravine where they would have privacy and the young man could target shoot.

After closing up the office, the two men mounted up, with Zack Traynor carrying a burlap sack. Reaching their destination, they dismounted, and Traynor dumped out the contents of the sack: a rope, several empty tin cans, and some whiskey bottles.

"All right, Will," said the marshal, "let me show you how you cock the hammer while drawing."

Will Hardin watched intently as his mentor drew the gun and cocked the hammer in slow motion, talking it through while in the process. "There has to be a perfect synchronizing of the thumb and fingers," the marshal instructed. "When your hand swings down, the thumb has to slip over the hammer and lever it back in the exact instant that the fingers secure a full grip on the butt. By the time the muzzle clears leather, the hammer has to be in firing position."

Traynor went through the process several times in slow motion, letting Cougar see the exact movement of arm, fingers, and thumb. When the student said he understood, the teacher told him to try it, and during the next half hour, Cougar improved smoothly and quickly.

The marshal then lined up several whiskey bottles on the trunk of a fallen tree. When the two men stood forty feet from the bottles, Traynor observed, "I already know how accurate you are when firing that rigged-up rifle of yours. But when drawing and firing a revolver as fast as you can, it's a whole new experience. Load your gun. Let's see what you can do."

It took Cougar Will Hardin only four tries before he hit the first bottle. Soon he was hitting a bottle in one out of three fast-draws. After another hour, he was not missing any.

Zack Traynor was enormously pleased with Cougar's prowess, and he decided to progress to a moving target. Tying the rope to an overhanging tree limb, he fastened a tin can to its end, then set the can in motion. Traynor backed up forty feet, drew lightning fast, and blew a hole through the center of the can. Turning to his pupil, he said, "Your turn."

Cougar laughed and said while shaking his head, "I'll never be that fast or that accurate, Zack."

The marshal grinned and replied, "You'll be faster and every bit as accurate, my boy. I can see it. You've got it in you."

Embarrassed by Traynor's overwhelming confidence in

him, Hardin blushed and mumbled, "I think you're patronizing me, just because I'm your deputy."

Traynor laughed. "Nope, it ain't so, kid. The good Lord just built you with great reflexes, a lean and powerful body that can move exceptionally fast, and a keen mind that is perfectly synchronized with your body. Trust me. You're a natural. Now, let's give it a try."

The marshal set the can in motion again, and Hardin shot off only one round without hitting the target. Reloading, he hit it twice in the next round and four times in the one after that. Traynor congratulated his student, telling him he was even more impressed than he had expected to be. Deciding Cougar had had enough practice for one day, the marshal told his deputy it was time to head back to town and become acquainted with the part of the job he was sure to dislike most: paperwork. As the two men remounted, Traynor told Hardin to ride out daily to the ravine and practice shooting.

When the week was finished, the two lawmen returned to the ravine together. "Okay. Show me what you've learned," the marshal instructed.

Will Hardin did as he was told, and Zack Traynor was astonished at his deputy's improvement. He was drawing much smoother and faster . . . and never once missed the swinging can.

"Okay, kid," Traynor said, walking ten paces away, then turning around, "now you're going to draw against me." When he saw the blank look come over Cougar's face, he chuckled, adding, "With empty guns."

Hardin's face relaxed and he grinned slowly. "Oh. For a minute there, I thought you'd lost your senses."

When both guns were empty and holstered, the two men, standing some thirty feet apart, took their stances. Then the marshal ordered, "Any time you're ready, Will, go for your gun."

Cougar waited for a few seconds, then his hand darted downward. Before he cleared leather, Traynor's gun was out, and the hammer slammed down on an empty chamber. "Bang! You're dead!" he chided.

Will Hardin blinked in disbelief. Shaking his head, he declared, "I didn't know I was that slow!"

"You're not, pal," replied the marshal. "You gave me the jump on you."

"I what?"

"You telegraphed your move. The expression in your eyes told me when you were going to go for your gun—and I simply went for mine when I saw it. You must learn to deaden your eyes when you're facing a man who intends to kill you. But be alert and try to read the signals in your *opponent's* eyes."

Cocking his head slightly, Hardin remarked, "I can barely *see* your eyes, much less read the signals in them."

Traynor grinned. "That's another little trick, my boy. Where's the sun?"

"In the sky."

"Okay, smart aleck. What's its position in the sky?"

"Directly behind you."

"So I can see your face quite plainly, but mine's in shadow, right?"

"Right. I get it. Always put the sun at my back, if I possibly can."

"Correct. Your life may depend on it. Now let's position ourselves so neither of us has the sun at our back and draw again."

With the next draw, Marshal Zack Traynor found himself bested by his student. Traynor was proud of Hardin and cautioned him to practice every day to keep himself sharp. "Now that you've got a badge on your chest," the older lawman warned, "you can expect to have to use your fast-draw skill at any time."

Sheridan's annual knife-throwing and shooting contest took place on the last day of May, and this year, as usual, a large crowd gathered for the event, with people coming from many miles around. Keeping his promise to Veronica

Simmons, Cougar Will Hardin went to the schoolhouse beforehand to give a special demonstration of his knife-throwing ability.

The children were restless with excitement as they stood outside, watching as the tall, slender man set a board with small pieces of paper pinned on it against a tree, then backed up several paces. Gasps of astonishment rose from Cougar's young audience as time after time he threw his knife at a piece of paper, each time splitting it in half. When the demonstration was over, Veronica was quick to point out to her students what diligent practice and determination could do. She had the children thank their guest in unison, then dismissed them to attend the contest.

Will Hardin always enjoyed Veronica's company, and he stayed for a few minutes, talking to her, while all the children except one scattered. Ten-year-old Kathy Welton, whose family's ranch was a good distance from town and who therefore boarded with her aunt during the week, had been told to stay at the schoolhouse until her parents came to get her. The girl, who now waited with her teacher as the schoolmarm talked with Sheridan's new deputy marshal, listened intently to the adults. Finally, Cougar told Veronica he would see her at the contest, and then he left.

Looking lovingly after Hardin's retreating back for a long moment, Veronica then turned to her pupil and said, "Well, Kathy, I wonder when your mother is going to get here. I can't go off and leave you alone."

"She'll be here soon, I'm sure, Miss Simmons," responded the freckle-faced girl, twirling one of her carrot-red braids. Kathy paused a moment, then asked, "Miss Simmons, could I ask you something?"

Bending over so as to be level with Kathy, Veronica replied, "Of course, dear. What is it?"

"I can see by the way you look at Mr. Cougar that you really like him a lot. Are you going to get married?"

Veronica blushed, caught completely unaware by the

bold question. She straightened, cleared her throat, and stammered, "Well . . . well, Kathy, you see—"

"Kathy!"

The little girl whirled around at the sound of her mother's voice. Sarah and Paul Welton and their son, Bobby, were seated in the family buckboard parked on the road at the front of the schoolyard. Relieved that their arrival meant she would not have to answer the question, Veronica took Kathy by the hand and led her to the buckboard. The young schoolteacher smiled to herself as she looked at her pupil's parents. Sarah Welton was a brunette, as was her son, but it was easy for anyone to see how Kathy had inherited her red hair. Her father's thick, shaggy hair was, if anything, even redder than his daughter's.

After greeting Veronica, Paul Welton helped Kathy onto the buckboard, then asked the girl, "You ready to go watch the contests, honey?"

"Sure am, Daddy," the child replied. "We already got to see Mr. Cougar throw his knife. I think he's going to win all the contests again this year."

"I wouldn't be surprised," Welton said with a laugh as Kathy settled on the seat beside her mother.

Sarah Welton asked Veronica, "Would you like to ride with us, Miss Simmons?"

"Thank you, Mrs. Welton," responded the young blonde, "but I have to close up the schoolhouse first. I'll be along shortly, though. I don't want to miss any of the contests."

"All right," Sarah said, smiling. "See you there."

Paul Welton clucked at the horses, and the buckboard wheeled away. Veronica smiled and waved, then walked back into the one-room building. As she put her papers into her desk drawer and tidied up, Veronica's heart was heavy. Sighing, she thought, *Kathy, you don't know how much I wish I could tell you that Cougar and I are going to be married. I long for his love more than anything in the world.*

*   *   *

Cougar Will Hardin was keenly aware of Veronica Simmons's presence among the nearly thirteen hundred people who had come to attend the contests. Along with his parents and his grandfather, Red Wolf, Veronica cheered him on as he handily won the knife-throwing and rifle-shooting events.

When it came time for the pistol-shooting contest, man after man was eliminated until it came down to a battle between Will Hardin and a husky stranger named Tex Finley.

While the crowd was cheering Cougar on, Finley leaned close to him and said, "Seems you're a big hero in these parts, Slim. Well, get ready, 'cause I'm just about to knock you off your pedestal."

Cougar eyed him steadily and retorted coolly, "Why don't you do it, *then* talk about it, mister?"

Tex Finley glared at his challenger, then grunted, "I will."

The competition in the pistol-shooting final was close, but Cougar Will Hardin came out the victor, and he was then declared the grand champion of the entire contest. While the crowd cheered and applauded, Tex Finley, looking disgusted, joined two friends who stood on the edge of the crowd.

Veronica Simmons gave her mother an excited hug, then dashed to the champion. Seeing her coming, Cougar welcomed her with a wide smile. She stood on her tiptoes and planted a kiss on his cheek, exclaiming, "Will, I'm so proud of you!"

Cougar kissed Veronica's cheek in turn, murmuring, "Thank you, Ronnie."

The winner's family pushed their way through the press to congratulate him. Dressed in her brightly colored Blackfoot regalia, Meadowlark embraced her tall, handsome stepson, kissed his cheek, and told him, "You did a great job, Will. Nobody can match my son!" Putting her head closer and speaking in a low voice, she confessed, "I'm especially glad that you beat out that unsavory-looking stranger. Your father and I decided between us that we didn't like the looks of that one—or either of his friends."

"Yeah, son," spoke up Obadiah, patting Cougar's back. "You did great, as usual. I'm glad you showed that fella up so handily."

After Red Wolf had offered his congratulatory words, he allowed the rest of the crowd to do the same. When the last of the well-wishers had spoken to him, Will Hardin started to move toward his parents, who stood nearby talking to the Simmonses. Suddenly Tex Finley blocked the victor's way, eyeing him with disdain, and when Cougar's friends and relatives noticed what was happening, they all stopped talking and watched carefully.

A sneer curled Finley's lip as he muttered, "I saw you huggin' that squaw, Slim. What are you, a dirty Indian lover? If I was you, I'd wash my face after bein' kissed by a filthy squaw."

Hearing the comment, Obadiah, a deep scowl on his face, started toward Finley, but Cougar put out a hand, holding his father at bay. Without taking his cold gray eyes off Finley, the young man said, "I'll take care of it, Pa." Obadiah was breathing hotly, but he gave in to his son's instructions.

Will Hardin felt as though his insides had turned to stone. His voice was low and dangerous as he held Finley with his icy gaze and growled, "That's my stepmother you've insulted, mister—and you're going to apologize to her for what you called her."

An imperious smirk settled on Finley's face. To his friends he said, "Hear that, boys? The deputy here has a filthy Indian for a mama. Kinda makes you wonder how the good folks of this fine town could want him for their lawman, don't it?"

With Hardin's face stiffened in anger, the veins in his neck stuck out like rope, while the color of his face deepened, leaving the white scars to stand out in contrast. Without warning, his right fist lashed out with the potency of a mule's kick, smashing into the hollow of Finley's unshaven jaw and sending the man rolling. His two friends began clawing for their guns, but Cougar immediately kicked one in the crotch, and the other one found himself looking down the black muzzle of the deputy's revolver before he could clear leather.

While the one man rolled on the ground, doubled over in agony, Red Wolf wrenched the gun from his hand. Veronica Simmons left her mother's side and rushed over to Meadowlark, putting a protective arm around her.

Tex Finley was swaying on his knees and shaking his head, trying to rise. His other friend stood wide-eyed as Cougar lined his revolver on the bridge of his nose and commanded, "Hand me your gun."

When the man had done so, Cougar tossed the gun to his father. "Watch him, Pa. If he moves, clout him a good one on the noggin."

Obadiah grinned and nodded. "It'd be my pleasure, son."

Holstering his own gun, Cougar glared at Finley as the man regained his feet. Storming over to him, planting his legs squarely with his arms folded across his sinewy chest, Will Hardin snarled, "Are you ready to apologize to my mother?"

Finley's face reflected his rebellion. But before he could speak, the deputy grabbed the front of his shirt and back-handed him repeatedly across the face with sharp, stinging blows. Finley tried to break Cougar's hold, but when he did not succeed, he swung a fist at his head. Releasing Finley's shirt, Cougar warded off the blow with an elbow, then decked his opponent with a right cross. Pouncing on him, the wiry lawman rolled Finley facedown on the ground, and although Finley tried to fight back, Cougar's hands and arms were as strong as steel. Furious at the man's loathesome behavior toward Meadowlark, Will Hardin rammed the man's face repeatedly and violently into the hard earth until blood spurted from his nose and sprayed from his mouth.

Tex Finley was moaning and gasping for breath as Will

Hardin yanked him to his feet, then sank his fingers into his lank hair and dragged him to where Meadowlark stood. Holding the man by the hair with one hand and by the seat of the pants with the other, Cougar rasped, "Okay, you miserable excuse for a human being, tell my mother you are sorry for what you said."

Clearly knowing it was useless to refuse and that to do so would only bring him more pain and injury, Tex Finley choked, "I . . . I'm sorry, ma'am. I shouldn't have said . . . what I did."

Shaking him hard enough to snap his neck, Cougar demanded, "Tell her *you* are the one who is dirty and filthy."

In fearful obedience, Finley repeated the words.

Satisfied, Cougar released him and snarled, "Take your pals and get out of my town, Finley. I was nice to you this time, but if I ever see hide or hair of you again, I won't be so considerate."

When the three strangers had gone, a young townsman who had been watching the fight came over to the deputy and clapped him on the back. "Remind me never to get on your wrong side, Will."

Cougar chuckled, then told him, "Well, Dave, just never lay hands or foul words on somebody I love, and you won't have anything to worry about."

Chapter Three

It was midmorning on June 12, 1883, and a warm breeze, pungent with the sweet scent of wildflowers, wafted across the Bighorn Mountains and in through the open windows of the Hardin house. With school out for the summer, Veronica Simmons often spent time with Meadowlark Hardin, and that morning was no exception. The two women sat on the big open, breezy porch, busy lacing braided rugs, while Will and Obadiah Hardin and Red Wolf were out back, in Cougar's old shop, finishing polishing fifty knives. The two older men were preparing to deliver them to the trading post in Sheridan and at the same time pick up food and other supplies.

The men's muted voices rode on the breeze, and from time to time the women turned their heads, catching a word or a phrase. Turning toward the schoolteacher, Meadowlark reached out and patted her hand. "I'm so glad to have your company—and I'm most pleased that Will is here at the same time."

Veronica sighed. "It doesn't seem to do much good, I'm afraid. I don't think he ever considers me as anything more than a friend"—she made a face—"or worse, a younger sister."

Meadowlark smiled encouragingly. "Give it time, child.

He loves you, I know he does." She laughed, adding, "Unfortunately *he* does not realize it as yet."

Just then the three men rounded the end of the porch, each holding a wooden box. Climbing onto the porch, Will Hardin lifted the lid of his box and pulled out one of the highly polished knives. He smiled at Veronica and asked, "Want to see one of my latest creations?"

"Yes, indeed." Reaching out, she took the knife in her hand. She turned it from side to side, looking at it admiringly, and murmured, "You always do such beautiful work, Will."

The deputy grinned with pleasure and replied, "They look as good as they do because of the way Pa and Grandpa polish them."

Chortling, Obadiah shook his head. "He's too humble a sort, isn't he, Veronica? Anyone with one eye and half sense can see the expert craftsmanship is there before Red Wolf and I ever touch them."

Will Hardin remained mute, merely smiling shyly. Replacing the knife in the box, he handed it over to his father.

Obadiah turned to his wife and said, "Meadowlark, darlin', Red Wolf and I are gonna hitch up the team and head for town now."

"You have a list of the things I need from the trading post?" asked the Indian woman.

"Yes'm," the big bearded man assured her, patting his shirt pocket.

Putting down her rug, Meadowlark stood and stepped in front of her husband. Taking his arm, she smiled up at Obadiah and commented, "You've been talking about getting a new pair of boots for six months. Don't you think it is time you broke down and did it?"

Obadiah looked down at his shabby, scuffed boots, the toes of which were worn thin. "I suppose you're right, honey-pot. Guess I'd better do it before winter, huh?"

She laughed. "Yes, I guess you had better." She gave him a loving hug, then released him and looked warmly at her stepson. "Where is it you are going when you leave here, Will?" she asked. "You said you have an errand to run for Marshal Traynor?"

The young deputy sighed. "Yes. I have to go arrest Chester Banks. He was in the Yellow Rose Saloon last night and got himself liquored up, then picked a fight with old Ezra Jones. You know Ezra. He never causes any trouble. But Chester hauled off and smacked him a good one, and when Ezra tried to defend himself, Chester beat him up. Nobody reported it until Doc Sibley was called to Ezra's house early this morning. Ezra's in pretty bad shape, and he's pressing charges. I've got to take Chester in and lock him up till the circuit judge comes through and they can meet in court."

Veronica touched Hardin's arm. Worry etched lines on her brow as she told him, "Will, please be careful. Everybody in these parts knows that Mr. Banks has a very hot temper."

"You sound like Mom," Cougar quipped with a laugh.

"The girl cares a lot about you, young man," spoke up Meadowlark, her eyes shining, glad for the opportunity to say something in Veronica's behalf.

Cougar patted the younger woman's hand affectionately. "I think a lot of her, too—and I promise I'll be careful, Ronnie." Then, after giving Meadowlark a quick hug, he bid everyone good-bye, untied his horse, mounted it, and rode off.

Moments later, Obadiah and Red Wolf drove out of the yard, leaving the two women alone. "Well," said Meadowlark, putting her arm around Veronica's slender waist, "let's finish this up, shall we? Then we can start on one for you."

"Oh, I'd love that!" exclaimed the young blonde. Veronica cast a longing glance over her shoulder in the direction that Will Hardin had taken, and she murmured, "Who knows? Perhaps it will be part of my dowry."

Sheridan's main street was busy at noontime as four foul-smelling buffalo hunters emerged from the Lone Pine

Saloon at the south edge of town, where they had gone an hour earlier. Now well liquored up, each man gripped a half-empty whiskey bottle in his hand. The men—who were not above stealing and plundering to get what they wanted—wore wide-brimmed, sweat-stained hats and filthy plaid shirts, and in spite of the summer's heat they were clad in buffalo-hide vests that not only had been poorly tanned but were rank with sweat. The combined human and animal smells exuded a fetid odor so foul as to render the men offensive to anyone they came near.

Their leader was a giant barrel-chested brute of a man named Gordo Silcox, whose massive sloping shoulders and arms were more like tree trunks than limbs. The beard around his mouth was tobacco-stained a dirty brown, and his weathered, sun-darkened skin resembled the bark of an oak tree. He had a broad nose, which had obviously been broken several times, and his small, black, narrow-set eyes more than suggested deadly menace.

The others of the group were no less unsavory than their leader. At twenty-six, Jonathan Silcox was two decades younger than his father. He was not quite Gordo's size, but resembled him remarkably . . . right down to his piglike, violent-looking eyes. Mel Goss, somewhere in his midthirties, was distinguished from his dirty, bearded companions only by his size—he was of medium height and build. The last of the foursome, George Lang, about the same age as Mel Goss, was tall and lean and had a bony, ratlike face that ably depicted his nature. Right next to Gordo Silcox in viciousness, Lang savored every opportunity to display his wicked nature.

Gordo Silcox spit a brown stream of tobacco juice into the dusty road, then gestured toward the trading post across the street with his bottle. "Let's get them supplies we need so's we can ride on."

While Silcox led his men into the street and headed for the trading post, George Lang stepped ahead and waved his arms at oncoming vehicles and riders, bringing traffic to a halt. "Everybody stop!" he bellowed. "Gordo the Great is crossin' the street!"

People looked on with disgust. An elderly rancher guiding his wagon along the street glared at them, shouting, "Drunken fools! Get out of the way!"

Defiantly, the buffalo hunters planted themselves in the middle of the road. The other three looked on amused as Lang approached the old man and snapped, "By the time a man gets to be your age, pop, he oughtta know enough to keep his trap shut!" Grabbing the oldster's hat, he pulled it off and poured whiskey over the driver's head. Lang roared with laughter as he replaced the hat, then joined his cohorts and headed into the trading post.

The elderly rancher, clearly knowing that to defend himself would incur further cruelty, watched them in stony silence. As soon as the men had passed from view, the oldster clucked to his team and headed for the marshal's office.

Reaching his destination, the rancher learned that Marshal Zack Traynor and Deputy Will Hardin had both been called out of town on business. With a sigh, resigned to the fact that the buffalo hunters' behavior would go undisciplined, the old man clucked to his team yet again and headed farther up the street.

The rowdies had been inside the trading post only minutes when Obadiah Hardin and Red Wolf hauled up in front and set the brake. As the two men alighted, Obadiah said, "Okay. Let's take these knives in, collect the money, and then pick up the stuff on Meadowlark's list."

"When are you going to get your new boots?" queried the wrinkled old Blackfoot.

"After everything else is taken care of," replied the mountain man.

Obviously determined to make sure his son-in-law got a new pair of boots, Red Wolf suggested, "We can save time if I take the knives in and pick up those things on the list while you go to the bootmaker."

Obadiah Hardin shrugged. "Fine." Reaching into the

pocket of his red plaid shirt, he produced his wife's list and handed it to his father-in-law, saying he would meet him back here shortly. Obadiah then hurried toward the boot shop nearly two blocks away, waving to a couple of friends across the street as he went.

Standing at the rear of the wagon, Red Wolf dropped the tailgate, and a loud belch sounded. The old Indian glanced briefly at the entrance of the trading post, noting the four unsavory-looking men who had just come through the door. Paying no attention to them, he reached into the wagon bed for one of the wooden boxes.

At that instant Gordo Silcox focused on Red Wolf. Biting off a fresh chaw of tobacco from a plug he had just stolen, he snorted mirthfully, then exclaimed, "Hey, boys! Lookee there! A stinkin', no-good redskin!"

Red Wolf was ready to hoist the weight of the box but paused as the foul-smelling men suddenly surrounded him, tossing their empty whiskey bottles into the dust.

Looking down at the small Blackfoot, Silcox's yellow teeth were bared in a cruel smirk. "Hey, boys," he asked, "remember them other stinkin' redskins? The ones that gave us trouble down by Laramie City?" Without waiting for a response, the giant continued, "They got away from us, but this one ain't gonna get away. We'll make *him* pay for what *they* did! After all, one stinkin' redskin's just like another."

Red Wolf's cheeks darkened with anger. His aging, milky eyes stared unwaveringly at the huge buffalo hunter as he told him firmly, "It would be best that you not bother me."

"Oh, yeah?" Silcox snickered, looking at the old Indian mockingly. "And why is that?"

"My grandson is deputy marshal of this town. He would become very angry if you give me trouble. Believe me, you do not want to feel the sharp edge of his temper."

George Lang laughed hollowly. Moving closer to Red Wolf, he snarled, "So this town's got a stupid redskin for a deputy marshal, eh? They must be purty hard up for lawmen around here!"

The old Indian ignored the slur. Picking up the wooden box, he started to push his way past them.

"Hey, hold on there!" Silcox bawled. "Whatcha got in that fancy box?"

"Nothing that is of any interest to you," clipped Red Wolf. "Now, I will thank you to move out of my way."

George Lang's face stiffened. Placing his hand against the old Indian's chest, he shoved him hard against the back of the wagon. "Hey, Indian!" he bellowed angrily. "That's no way for you to talk to Gordo the Great! I think you'd better apologize! Now!"

His voice as brittle as winter ice, Red Wolf snapped, "I have nothing for which to apologize!" As he spoke he tried again to shove his way past Lang.

Lang merely pressed him tighter against the wagon, saying to his leader, "I think we need to see what's in the box, Gordo."

"Me, too," agreed the massive man, grabbing the box. "Gimme that, Indian!"

Red Wolf jerked the box free and clutched it to his chest. But Silcox brought a huge hamlike fist down onto the box, jarring it loose from the old Blackfoot's fingers, and it crashed to the ground. The lid popped open, and many of the knives scattered, their shiny steel blades gleaming in the sunlight.

"Hey look, Pa! Knives!" shouted Jonathan Silcox, who was a tad slow mentally.

The elder Silcox and the others picked up the knives and looked them over with admiration. Each ruffian commented on their beauty and the precision of their balance.

George Lang noted the paw print etched on the handles and demanded, "Hey, Indian, what's this cat's paw on here for?"

"The knives are made by my grandson," the old Indian replied proudly. "His nickname is Cougar—and believe me, you do not want to anger him. Place the knives back in the box, and go your way."

"No way, Geronimo," rasped Lang, shaking his head vigorously. "I want a couple of these for myself." Looking at the gang leader, he proposed, "Gordo, let's keep what we want of these and sell off the rest. Knives like these will bring a purty penny!"

"Good idea, George," the huge man agreed. "Let's do it."

Red Wolf's anger had mounted steadily within him, and he had borne all he could. Doubling up both fists, he cracked Lang on the jaw with one and pounded him in the ribs with the other. But the blows barely made an impact, and Lang countered with a violent punch to the old man's kidney. Red Wolf stiffened, then fell.

When the Indian hit the ground, Mel Goss kicked him savagely in the face and chest, while George Lang stood over him, a menacing figure in the bright sunlight. Shoving Goss aside, he cursed and snapped, "Outta my way, Mel! Let me at him!"

Lang drew back his right foot and sent a violent kick to Red Wolf's stomach. There was a whoosh of escaping air from the Blackfoot's mouth, followed by a groan. His eyes filled with agony, Red Wolf nonetheless looked unwaveringly at Lang, but that only seemed to infuriate the buffalo hunter even further, and Lang swore again and sent a harder kick to the same spot. The Indian grunted weakly and went limp.

"Oh, no, you don't, old man!" blustered Lang, bending over and sinking his fingers into Red Wolf's shirt. "You don't go out cold on me yet!"

He jerked the frail body upright. Red Wolf was not unconscious, but his eyes were glazed and his head lolled to one side. His lips were split and bleeding, and there were numerous bruises on his leathery face. Lang held him easily with one hand and pulled back the other. But before he could unleash the blow, Jonathan Silcox grinned and chopped the Indian hard on the back of the neck. Red Wolf sagged and went unconscious in George Lang's hand.

Dropping Red Wolf into the dirt, Lang charged after Jonathan, shouting. "You stupid numskull! He was mine! He didn't punch you!"

Jonathan braced himself for an onslaught, but Lang was stopped dead in his tracks as Gordo Silcox grabbed him by the collar. "Hey! Leave my son alone!" blared the giant. "Besides, what difference does it make? The Indian's a bloody mess, and that's all that counts. C'mon. Let's go sell them knives."

George Lang's wrath cooled quickly in the face of his cohort's massive presence. Grinning, his feral face somewhat submissive, Lang said quickly, "Sure, Gordo. Let's make us some money."

Stepping over Red Wolf's crumpled, unmoving form, the buffalo hunters gathered up the spilled knives and put them back in the box, then grabbed the other two boxes from the wagon bed. Silcox suggested, "Let's go to the Yellow Rose Saloon. There'll be more men in there than in the Bighorn. When we're done there, we can go over to the Bighorn—if we've got any of these knives left." He laughed gleefully, adding, "We're gonna make us a bundle, fellas!"

Chapter Four

Rancher Chester Banks was an ill-tempered loner who seemed to have a grudge against the world. It took very little to ignite his wrath, and usually when he ventured into town, he ended up angry with someone. Last night Ezra Jones had become the target of that anger.

It was early afternoon, and as Deputy Marshal Will Hardin rode down the road toward Banks's ranch, he saw the big, blocky man setting a new post for his corral gate. Sweat dripped from the rancher's face as he tamped the dirt around the base of the post with an iron bar.

Banks had obviously heard Hardin's approach, for he stopped what he was doing and turned to watch him draw near, leaning the iron bar against the post. He then removed his hat and pulled a dirty bandanna from a hip pocket to mop his face. The young deputy hoped there would be no trouble with Banks, but the man's reputation made that prospect unlikely, and Cougar felt his body tensing reflexively as he rode ever closer.

Drawing up to the rancher, he set steely eyes on Banks and told him, "Chester, I'm here on business. Serious business."

Banks dropped his hat back on his head and looked at the lawman through dull, insolent eyes. "Don't bother to leave your saddle, Hardin," he said brusquely. "We've got nothing to talk about."

Dismounting in spite of the rancher's words, Will Hardin stepped close to him and retorted, "I didn't come here to talk. I came here to arrest you for assaulting Ezra Jones. There were plenty of witnesses at the Yellow Rose who saw what you did to him, so you can't lie your way out of it."

Bristling, Banks set his jaw and snapped, "I don't need to lie about anything. That fight was—"

"You're under arrest!" blared Cougar, his own words cutting sharply across Banks's. "Ezra is pressing charges for assault and battery, and I have a warrant. Get your horse, 'cause we're going to town where you'll stay locked up until you and Ezra meet in court."

Banks's mouth pulled down angrily, and his muscular shoulders tightened while his suntanned face grew hard. His voice was stubborn as he said, "You're not locking me up, Hardin."

The lawman regarded the rancher levelly for a moment, then responded, "That's where you're wrong, Chester. Now, you can come the easy way, or you can come the hard way. But either way I'm taking you in."

Cougar saw the fire ignite in the stocky man's eyes. Banks made a sudden turn and grasped the iron tamping bar, but Will Hardin's move was even faster, and he seized the bar before the rancher had a tight grip on it, wrenching it from him. Tossing it away, he snapped, "That's enough, Banks! Don't make me have to get tough. Go get your horse."

Banks's voice was challenging as he roared, "I've never been behind bars in all my life, and it's not gonna happen now!"

As he spoke, the rancher swung a meaty fist toward Cougar's jaw. But the agile deputy stepped aside and threw a punch of his own. His iron-hard fist connected with Banks's jaw, and the rancher staggered back, surprised. Before he could regain his balance, he was peppered with rights and lefts that whipped his head both ways, wearing him down.

Banks slipped to the ground with glazed eyes and a muddled brain. He sat groaning and muttering while Hardin's strong hands grabbed his arms, jerking them unmercifully behind him. The click of steel ratchets being snapped shut sounded loudly as handcuffs were clamped around the man's wrists.

Cougar took hold of Chester Banks's collar and hoisted him to his feet. Banks swayed a bit, his head obviously spinning. "Okay, Banks, let's go to the barn and get your horse," the young lawman commanded. "Like I said, I'm taking you in."

Breathing hard and blinking repeatedly to clear his vision, Banks whined, "I don't have time to sit in jail. There's work around here that has to be done."

"You should've considered that before you cut loose on Ezra Jones last night—a man considerably smaller than you are and a good ten years older, besides."

"I was drunk," Banks whined.

"Tell it to the judge," Cougar parried. "Come on. Let's go."

After roughly getting the shackled rancher onto his horse, Deputy Hardin led his prisoner toward town. A half hour later, the Simmons house and outbuildings, set back a good distance from the road among the trees, came into view. As the riders passed alongside the fence, Cougar saw Dale Simmons and a ranch hand working on a bull calf that was on its feet but was obviously ill and weak.

Simmons was straddling the calf and holding its jaws open while his hired man was attempting to pour medicine from a dark-colored bottle into the young animal's mouth. But the calf balked at the help, bawling and spraying the man with the medicine.

Drawing to a halt just outside the fence, Cougar called to Simmons, "Sick calf?"

Simmons first flicked a glance at his shackled neighbor, then looked at Hardin and replied, "Yeah. He's got the scours." Looking back and forth between the two men, Simmons then asked, "What's Chester done?"

The deputy explained why Banks was under arrest, adding, "He'll be cooling his heels in jail until the judge comes through and a trial can be held." Gesturing toward the calf, Cougar then queried, "What's that you're trying to give that little fella?"

"Some medicine Doc Sibley gave me. He said it works good on humans with the same problem, so he figured it might work on a calf."

"I'll tell you something that will work for sure," Will Hardin remarked, "and he won't put up such a fuss getting it down his throat."

"What's that?"

"Oh, a little remedy my grandpa Red Wolf taught me. Works every time. It'll stop the diarrhea in a couple of days."

Simmons grinned. "I'm all ears."

"Pour raw egg down his throat twice a day—after taking it out of the shell, of course," he added with a laugh. "Mix the egg white and yolk up good in a cup, then straddle him, hold his jaws apart, and pour in the egg. It'll slide down real quick and go to work on his innards. You'll see. Grandpa knows what he's talking about."

"I don't doubt it for a minute," Dale Simmons responded. "We'll take this little guy up to the house right now and give him Red Wolf's remedy. Thanks for the information."

"I'll send you my bill," Cougar quipped as he rode away, leading Chester Banks's horse.

Arriving in Sheridan, Cougar Will Hardin headed for the jail, noting the passersby staring at his handcuffed prisoner. The deputy reached his destination and saw the sign tacked up by Zack Traynor on the office door saying he was not in. Starting to dismount at the hitch rail, Hardin heard his name being called and looked over to see a man running up the street from the other side of town.

Panting hard, the man drew up and gasped, "Cougar! Some . . . some buffalo hunters just beat up your grandpa! I mean . . . they hurt him real . . . bad! He's up by . . . the tradin' post!"

"Where's my pa? Is he with Red Wolf?" asked the deputy, his face losing color.

"I don't know. All's I know is your . . . grandpa needs help real quick. Someone went for Doc Sibley . . . and I was comin' to get the marshal." He looked over and saw the note, then added, "But I guess he ain't around." Catching his breath, the man commented, "Sure's a good thing you came when you did."

Acting quickly, Cougar jerked Chester Banks off his horse and hustled him inside the office. He practically dragged the man to one of the cells, unlocked the handcuffs, then hurried out, slamming the barred door behind him. After giving the key a quick turn, Will Hardin shoved it into his pocket and raced out of the office toward the trading post.

Running as fast as he could, the lanky deputy came within sight of the scene and saw his father kneeling over Red Wolf, who was stretched out on the ground beside the family wagon. A small crowd was gathered around the two men.

Kneeling beside his father, Cougar gasped at the sight of the battered and blood-smeared face of the old Indian. Without looking at his son, Obadiah hissed, "Buffalo hunters."

"Yeah," Cougar breathed. "That's what I was told."

The deputy pulled out his bandanna and gently wiped away some of the blood. Red Wolf was conscious, but his eyes were glazed, and the younger Hardin asked softly, "Grandpa, can you tell me what the men looked like and how many there were?"

Red Wolf ran a dry tongue over equally dry lips, but although he was clearly trying hard to talk, he could only manage a squeak.

A man who stood nearby said, "There were four of 'em,

Will. Some of us were in the Lone Pine a while ago when they came in there. Filthy bunch. Stunk the place up good. The leader's a giant, and I heard the others call him Gordo."

Another man offered, "They started pickin' on Red Wolf because he's an Indian. They also took your knives and said they were gonna sell 'em. That's when your grand-daddy lit into 'em."

Will Hardin looked around, then told his father, "Pa, since Doc Sibley hasn't gotten here yet, you take Grandpa over to his office. I'm going to find the scum who did this."

"It won't be hard to do, Will," came the voice of an-other man in the crowd. "They're up at the Yellow Rose right now."

"Thanks, Alex," Cougar responded.

"I'll go after them with you, son," Obadiah said.

Shaking his head, Cougar replied, "No, Pa. I'll handle it. You just get Grandpa to Doc Sibley." Then, leaning close to the old man, he said comfortingly, "You'll be all right, Grandpa. Doc'll fix you up—and I'll fix those dirty skunks for what they did to you."

Red Wolf nodded slowly, closing his eyes. He was obvi-ously in pain.

Looking to the men in the crowd as he rose to his feet, Will Hardin asked for a more detailed description of the buffalo hunters. Then he strode stiffly upstreet toward the Yellow Rose Saloon, his insides burning with wrath.

Gordo Silcox and his cohorts stood at the bar in the Yellow Rose Saloon, drinking and showing off the shiny knives to the other patrons. As many of the men in the saloon were transients on their way to or from Montana, they were unaware that the knives were made locally and were sold at the trading post at the other end of town.

Silcox held one of the precision-made knives in his huge hand, waved it about with a flourish, and exclaimed, "You've never seen anything like 'em, gentlemen! They're balanced perfectly, and they're so sharp you can shave with 'em"—he grinned, pausing for effect—"without soap!"

Several patrons came closer for a better look. One of them asked, "Who makes 'em, mister?"

The giant looked at him blankly for a second, then flashed the handle, exposing the cougar paw insignia, and answered, "They . . . uh . . . they're made by the Catpaw Knife Company down in . . . uh . . . Laramie City. See that mark? That's their mark. A paw print."

"Them's right nice goods," spoke up another, his eagerness evident. "How much?"

Silcox grinned, answering, "Well, they usually sell for fifteen dollars but—"

"That's awful high, mister!" retorted the man. "This here knife on my waist is a good one, and it only cost five dollars."

"It's inferior compared to these knives," the buffalo hunter countered. "But I tell you what. I'm feelin' generous today, so instead of fifteen, I'll let these go for twelve! How's that?"

Several of the patrons responded by pulling out their money, but before they handed it over, one of Sheridan's citizens stepped over and said sharply, "This guy's takin' you men! These knives are made right here in town by our deputy marshal, Will Hardin. His nickname's Cougar, and that's *his* mark on the handles. And what's more, you can buy 'em at our tradin' post at the other end of the street for ten dollars!"

Silcox's face flushed angrily. Raking the man with a hot glare, he growled, "You're stickin' your nose in where it don't belong, mister! I'd advise you to mind your own business, or you'll live to regret it!"

"You're the one who's got regrets coming!" Cougar Will Hardin suddenly shouted from the doorway, where he had been watching and listening.

Everyone in the saloon turned toward the angry voice. The deputy stood silhouetted in the doorway with the sun-bleached street at his back, while his hands held the batwings halfway open.

Gordo Silcox looked the wiry young lawman up and down, his glance resting momentarily on the badge on Hardin's chest.

Cougar shoved through the doors, glaring at the buffalo hunters. The room was ominously quiet, and the squeaking of the swinging batwings seemed unnaturally loud. Hardin's steely gaze settled on Gordo Silcox, and as he regarded the huge man, he asked raggedly, "Where'd you get those knives?"

The men who were gathered at the bar slowly backed away, leaving only the four buffalo hunters in a tight knot. The barkeep spoke from behind the bar, pleading, "Cougar, don't tear my place up, okay?"

The deputy's intent focus was on the ruffians before him, and he did not reply to the bartender. Rather, he walked closer to the gang leader and snapped, "I asked where you got those knives, mister—and I want an answer!"

George Lang regarded the wiry lawman with amusement, and he told Silcox softly, "He's all alone. Let's take him."

Silcox shifted his glance from Cougar to the other men who stood around silently watching. Looking back at the deputy, he finally replied stiffly, "I got 'em down in Laramie City, where they're made."

Hardin's retort came like the snap of a whip. "*You're a liar!* You stole them from my grandfather, and then you beat him up! You beat up a defenseless old man to get them! You're not only a liar, you're a snake-bellied, yellow-spined coward—you and those cockroaches you pal around with!"

Goss, Lang, and the younger Silcox looked to their leader, waiting for his next move. Gordo Silcox's enormous chest was heaving, and it was obvious that he was feeling the pressure of having to stand up to Will Hardin in front of his cohorts. The young deputy's words were clearly a challenge, meaning there had to be retaliation.

Cougar ordered, "Drop your gun belts! You men are under arrest for assaulting an old man and for stealing my knives!"

Abruptly Silcox shouted, "Let's take him, boys!" and he charged Cougar.

The other three were not yet in motion as Cougar lithely sidestepped the thundering bulk of Gordo Silcox, then shoved him with all his might from behind, letting the man's momentum hurl him toward the wall. When the giant slammed into it headfirst, the impact shook the building, and Silcox fell in a heap, unconscious.

Mel Goss and George Lang were coming at the deputy shoulder to shoulder, their fists pumping, while Jonathan Silcox turned toward the bar and reached for a bottle to use as a club on the lawman.

Cougar turned himself into a human bowling ball, hitting the floor and spinning into the two men, who both went down, cursing loudly. The young deputy was instantly on his feet, his eyes dancing with excitement. These men were going to pay for what they had done to Red Wolf—and pay dearly.

Lang was recovering his footing first. But before he had completely righted himself, the wiry lawman chopped him with a violent punch, knocking him over a table and into a group of men who were hugging a wall to keep out of the way. Two of them fell on top of the skinny buffalo hunter, pinning him.

Jonathan Silcox set his mouth in a firm line and hefted the whiskey bottle. Cougar saw him coming, but he was about to get hit by Mel Goss, who was on his feet and charging. Adeptly, Hardin dodged Goss's fists, grabbed his hat by the brim, and pulled the man's head down as he brought his knee up solidly into Goss's chin. Nose gristle cracked, and when Hardin released his hold on the man, Goss fell backward, screaming in pain as he hit the floor hard.

Jonathan Silcox came lumbering in, swinging the bottle toward the back of Cougar's head. The deputy turned to meet the huge young man and was not able to dodge the bottle, which struck him on the right shoulder, sending splinters of pain down his arm and across his back. He staggered momentarily, then righted himself as Jonathan swung the bottle again. Ducking the weapon, Cougar drove a hard punch into the ruffian's midsection, and Jonathan buckled, his breath whooshing out of him. Before the young man could recover, Cougar chopped him with a sledgehammer blow to the hollow of his fleshy jaw. He hit the floor with a crash, out cold, and the bottle went down with him, shattering and spilling whiskey in every direction.

George Lang had shoved the men off him and was now on his feet, staggering toward the deputy and clawing for his gun. His voice slightly slurred, he railed, "I'm gonna kill you, lawman!"

Lang suddenly froze in his tracks as his fingers closed around the butt of his gun, for his opponent's revolver was in his hand, cocked, and pointed at Lang's heart.

"Leave it right there!" Cougar warned. "Pull it any farther and you're a dead man!"

Lang's face blanched, and he let go of the gun immediately.

With the help of several of the patrons, the buffalo hunters were disarmed. When Gordo Silcox came to, Deputy Will Hardin forced him to pay the bartender for damages. As the foursome was led out of the saloon past the snickering patrons, Silcox muttered that he would repay the young deputy for the humiliation Cougar had caused him.

Reaching the marshal's office, Will Hardin saw Zack Traynor riding in from the south. He explained all that had happened, and together the lawmen escorted the unsavory characters inside. They locked them in two separate cells, forcing Chester Banks to share his with two of the foul-smelling ruffians, and then they hurried up the street to Dr. Ben Sibley's office, eager to find out about Red Wolf's condition.

Obadiah Hardin was pacing in the waiting room when

they reached the clinic. Almost before Cougar could ask his father about Red Wolf, the doctor appeared, telling the men that the old Blackfoot would be all right. He had bruised ribs from being kicked, and Sibley had sewn up some cuts, but the stitches could come out within a week, and the bruises would heal. Sibley said in a voice filled with amazement and admiration, "He's quite something, that old man. That kind of a beating would have killed a lot of men far younger than he." He smiled, adding, "You can take him home with you right now."

Grateful that the Blackfoot had incurred no permanent damage, Obadiah and Will Hardin placed the old man in the family wagon, and the older Hardin took Red Wolf back to their mountain cabin.

As soon as the prisoners were alone, Gordo Silcox looked through the bars at Mel Goss and George Lang. "That skinny lawman is gonna die for humiliatin' us so bad!" he snarled. "Look what he did to us! We look like we've been through a war!"

"What're we gonna do, Gordo?" asked George Lang, rubbing his sore jaw.

"He can't hold us long," responded Silcox. "When he lets us out, we'll make like we're leavin' town, then double back. He's gonna get it but good."

"Maybe we'd better plan an ambush, Gordo," spoke up George Lang. "I ain't never seen a man pull iron so fast."

"We'll plan on how to do it after we get out," the huge man remarked. "One way or another, that deputy is gonna get it." As if suddenly aware of Chester Banks's presence, he glared at the other prisoner and warned, "You better not say nothin' about what you just heard if you want to remain alive, mister."

Shrugging, the rancher remarked, "On the contrary, I'm all for your plan. And your friend's right. Ambushing him'd be best. I'd suggest getting him when he's on his way to his parents' place."

The hostility in Gordo Silcox's eyes faded away, and

he looked at the rancher with interest. "Tell me more, partner."

Chester Banks told the buffalo hunters about Will Hardin's arresting him—and the pleasure it would give him to see the man get some retribution. "Cougar's ma and pa, along with the old Indian, live up in the Bighorns a few miles," he explained, "and he rides up there two or three times a week. So if you're patient and camp out in the right spot, he'll ride right into your lap."

Silcox's small, wicked eyes lit up. "You're makin' good sense, pal," he told Banks. "You know where his folks' house is?"

Nodding with satisfaction, Banks described how to find Obadiah Hardin's place. When he had finished, he offered, "I'd better warn you fellas of something. If you're going after Cougar, just be sure you get him—and I mean make it permanent. You don't want Cougar Will Hardin trailing you, 'cause he's better at tracking than any bloodhound or Indian you ever heard of. The man's uncanny. He could trail a flat-footed Indian over a mountain of smooth stone. If you're going after him, just don't mess up—'cause if you get him on your trail, he's got you." Banks then nodded at Lang, adding, "And you're right. If you're gonna take him, it'll have to be an ambush. I've never seen anybody fight the way he does."

"Where'd he learn to fight?" queried Lang.

"I'm sure his pa taught him the basics," responded Banks. "But most of what he knows just comes natural."

Gordo Silcox reached in his pocket and pulled out his chewing tobacco. He bit off a chaw, looking thoughtful for a long moment. Then he told the rancher, " 'Preciate all this information. We're beholdin' to you."

Banks gingerly touched his swollen face, then grunted, "You don't owe me a thing. Just get him."

Soon after arriving at the office the next morning, Deputy Will Hardin said to the marshal, "Zack, if it's all right with you, I think I'll turn those buffalo hunters loose.

They're stinking up our nice clean jail. Since my grandfather isn't hurt bad and I got my knives back, I'd like to just flat get rid of them."

"Suits me," Traynor agreed, grinning. "It smells worse than an outhouse back there." His face became serious as he added, "But make sure they know they're to get their tails out of this county and never return."

"I'll tell them that with pleasure," Cougar assured him.

A short time later the four men were released from the jail. Their weapons were returned, and with a look of disgust on his face, Cougar watched the scraggly bunch ride south out of town. "Good riddance," he muttered, waiting until they had passed from view. Then, satisfied that justice had been done, he turned and went back inside.

Chapter Five

The morning was clear and warm as Veronica Simmons emerged from the schoolhouse, carrying a stack of new textbooks. She had received word a short time earlier of the books' arrival from back East, and she had immediately gone into town to look them over. Having taken a copy of each, she was bringing them home to study, in preparation for the new term in September.

Veronica was dressed in riding breeches, a white, ruffled blouse, flat-crowned hat, and western-style boots, and she cut quite a figure as she placed the books in her saddlebags, then swung onto her dappled mare. Greeting people along the street as she rode, the beautiful blonde headed for the marshal's office. Spotting Will Hardin's horse in front of it, she felt her heart begin to beat faster, and it positively leapt when she saw the tall, handsome deputy step outside with Marshal Zack Traynor. Cougar was about to place a foot in a stirrup when he noticed Veronica, and when he smiled at her, Veronica's heart leapt yet again.

She called cheerfully, "Good morning, Will . . . Marshal Traynor."

Both men greeted her, and when the deputy asked her where she was off to, she told him, "After I drop off some books at home, I'm going to your parents' place. Meadowlark asked me to come back to continue working on the rug we started when I was there a couple of days ago."

"Hey, that's great!" exclaimed Hardin, who always showed interest in whatever Veronica was doing. "Are you going to be there for supper?"

Smiling, the schoolteacher answered, "It just so happens your mother invited me."

"Good! Me, too. If you like, I could ride you back to your ranch after supper."

Veronica felt as though her blood had risen in temperature. Remaining outwardly calm, she smiled again and said, "That would be very nice."

"Fine. Well, I'll see you later, then," he said, mounting his horse. "I've got to ride up to Bingham on an errand for Zack right now, but I'll be back in time for supper." He laughed, adding, "After eating my own cooking of late, one of Mom's meals will be quite a treat."

Knowing Bingham was some twenty miles to the northwest, Veronica noted, "That's a long ride. Are you sure you'll make it by then?"

"I'll make it, all right," he responded, grinning in the crooked way that always sent a chill down her spine.

"Well, okay, see you then," she said, giving him a little wave.

"Right. And I'll see you tomorrow, boss," Cougar said to Traynor.

Cougar had just touched his spurs to his horse's flanks and started up the street when Veronica called out suddenly, "Will!"

Hardin drew rein and waited as she trotted toward him. Drawing up, she spoke softly, "My father said to tell you that the egg remedy is working for the calf." Sighing, she added, "I think you must know everything, Deputy Hardin."

"Not quite, Miss Simmons," he replied, his tone ironic, "but what I *do* know, I owe to Pa, Mom, and Grandpa."

"Seems you've picked up a little on your own, too," she said with admiration.

"Maybe," he responded somewhat shyly, smoothing his

mustache. "Well, see you later, Ronnie." Once again putting his horse into a trot, he headed northward.

Veronica watched him until he passed from view, then dismounted at the hitch rail in front of the general store, two doors down from the marshal's office. Stepping onto the boardwalk, she was greeted by Max Slone, the proprietor, who had been sweeping the planking in front of his shop.

The shopkeeper followed Veronica into the store. They chatted for a few moments, and then she made a small purchase. As she turned to leave, Slone asked, "Think it'll ever come to be?"

She halted, then pivoted and inquired, "That what will ever come to be?"

"You and Cougar."

Veronica's fair skin colored. "What do you mean?" she asked in a hesitant voice.

"Honey, it's as clear as day how you feel about that man. But he just hasn't noticed you yet, has he?"

She was silent for a moment, then sighed and admitted, "Well, at least he considers me his best friend."

Slone chuckled, shaking his head. "Best friend, eh? The poor boy's got blinders on. I wonder what it'll take to get them off."

"I don't know," Veronica said with another sigh. "But I'm staying close by in case it ever happens." Her face brightened, and she remarked, "At least I get to eat supper with him at the Hardins' place this evening."

"Well, good luck," Slone offered.

Veronica thanked him and left the store. She untied her horse from the hitch rail, mounted up, and guided the mare toward the end of town. As she passed the marshal's office, Zack Traynor was leaving. He waved at her as he climbed onto his horse, then headed in the opposite direction. Idly wondering what business the lawman was attending to, the young schoolteacher adjusted the chin strap on her hat and rode out of town toward the magnificent Bighorn Mountains.

* * *

Gordo Silcox and his men had camped in the hills to the south of Sheridan, and as they sat eating beans and drinking coffee, Silcox looked at his cohorts and said, "The smart thing for us to do is wait near the edge of town and send Mel in to watch the marshal's office. From what that rancher told us, Hardin sometimes rides to his parents' place. We just gotta be patient, and when he goes next time, it'll be his *last* time."

Jonathan Silcox looked at his father and asked petulantly, "How come Mel gets to be the one to go into town and do the watchin', Pa?"

"Because he can't hardly do it without somebody seein' him . . . and he's the least obvious of any of us."

"I don't understand," Jonathan muttered, cocking his head and looking at the elder Silcox for further explanation.

"It's simple, Jonathan," George Lang put in. "You and your dad are so big, a blind man could spot you. I'm real tall and thin and kinda obvious to spot, too. Mel's just average size and build, with nothin' particularly special about him, so people won't notice him so easy."

Jonathan nodded, and a wide grin spread over his broad face. Chuckling, he said, "Right. You're special to look at, George, 'cause you look like a rat. Ain't too many men look like rats."

Lang's jaw tightened, and his face darkened. Leaping to his feet, he stepped to where Jonathan sat and stood over him, breathing hotly. "I told you never to say that about me again!" he bellowed. "I don't jab at you for bein' thick-headed and stupid, so don't you tell me I look like a rat! You say anything one more time, and so help me, I'll—"

"That's enough!" bawled Silcox, his powerful voice echoing through the surrounding woods. "You two knock it off! We got more important things to do—like find out when he's headed for his folks' place. I want to make sure we're waitin' for him when that deputy heads up into the mountains."

* * *

It was nearing ten o'clock when the ruffians drew up and dismounted in a brush-covered gully close by the southern end of Sheridan. The day was getting hot, and the men sat down in the shade while a plan was formed. It was decided that Mel Goss would make his way to a spot across the street from the marshal's office and keep watch, and if he did not see Cougar soon, he was to ask someone if the deputy was around. Once Goss learned the young lawman's whereabouts, he was to observe him. When Will Hardin headed out of town, Goss was to hurry back to the gully and advise Gordo Silcox.

Goss mounted up, and several minutes later he was tying his horse in front of Sheridan's bank. The street was a beehive of activity, and the mangy-looking buffalo hunter casually made his way along the boardwalk until he was directly across from the marshal's office. No one seemed to recognize him as he stepped into the shade of a doorway, then stood and watched the marshal's office, which seemed to be closed up.

Goss waited for nearly a half hour, and still there was no activity at the marshal's office. When the proprietor of the general store a couple of doors up from the office came out and began to arrange some barrels in front of his shop, the ruffian decided to ask the storekeeper if he knew the whereabouts of the marshal and his deputy. Threading his way through the traffic, he crossed the street and approached Max Slone.

Slone looked up and smiled. "Good morning, stranger," he said cheerfully.

"I wonder if you could help me," Goss responded in his most polite voice.

"I'll try," replied Slone, halting in his work.

"I was lookin' for the deputy marshal, Mr. Hardin. He's come many a time to my tradin' post south of here, sellin' me those beautiful knives of his, and I'm in need of a new supply. I found myself in his neck of the woods, and I thought I'd get some while I'm here. You know where he might be?"

The unsuspecting merchant told Goss that he had seen Will Hardin ride out of town earlier, but he had talked to Hardin's lady friend, Veronica Simmons, and she had mentioned that she and Hardin were going to spend some time together at his parents' place in the mountains.

Playing ignorant, Goss asked for directions to the Hardin place. After Slone had explained how to find Obadiah's cabin, Goss said casually, "I didn't see no one in the marshal's office. Ain't he around either?"

Shaking his head, the shopkeeper replied, "I heard Marshal Traynor tell Veronica that he had to go over to a nearby ranch. I believe he said something about stolen cattle."

Goss shook his head slowly. "Stealin' other folks' property . . ." he murmured. "It makes a body sad to remember that there's so much wickedness in the world." The ruffian then thanked Slone and beelined back to the gully where the others waited.

When Gordo Silcox heard Goss's story, he grinned evilly and declared, "So Cougar has a girlfriend, eh? That's interestin'. Well, they're probably both at the cabin by now, but we'll give 'em some time together . . . since it's the last time together they're gonna have!"

The others guffawed loudly, then Silcox remarked, "Since there ain't no lawmen hanging around, let's go into town and get us a couple of drinks. Then we'll head for the mountains."

Climbing onto their horses, the unsavory bunch headed for the Bighorn Saloon. They had been sitting at a table and drinking for about twenty minutes when some townsmen came in, bought drinks, and sat down nearby. Earl Vine, Jerrold Kohler, and Ned Bauer sipped at their whiskey and looked around. Earl Vine suddenly signaled his companions and pointed at the buffalo hunters, and it was obvious that the townsmen recognized the foursome as the men who had beaten up Red Wolf. Almost immediately, the smile on each of their faces was replaced by a sour look.

George Lang took note of the expressions of disgust being directed at him and his cronies and confronted the three patrons, demanding, "You fellas got a problem?"

Vine, the largest of the group, got to his feet and replied tartly, "We didn't until you and your pals came in. Now it stinks in here."

"Yeah," said Kohler, standing as well, "in more ways than one."

The other patrons and the bartender exchanged nervous glances as Lang's cohorts jumped to their feet, their faces red with anger. Bauer also rose as Gordo Silcox stomped over to Kohler and snapped, "Maybe you'd like to remove the stink by throwin' us out! Wanna try it?"

Ned Bauer's face reflected his fear. "Look, guys," he said quietly to his companions, "we're outnumbered here. Let's just vacate the place."

"Too late for that!" growled the huge buffalo hunter, swinging a meaty fist and connecting with Bauer's jaw, knocking him over a nearby table.

Shouting angrily, Earl Vine unleashed a punch at Silcox in return, but he found that it had little effect. Then the giant pulled out his pistol and cracked Vine across the face with it.

The other ruffians began pounding on Jerrold Kohler, flattening him. While his friend was bearing the brunt of the attack, Ed Bauer recovered and dashed out the door, intending to bring the marshal.

Vine went down from the pistol-whipping, but after a moment or two he got up, shaking his head and grabbing for his own gun. Gordo Silcox then swung his pistol in a wide arc and bashed Vine savagely on the head, and the man crumpled in a heap.

When he turned back to the others, Silcox found that his men had beaten Jerrold Kohler into unconsciousness. Holstering his weapon, he then ordered, "We'd better vamoose, boys."

The buffalo hunters strode past the bartender and the few other customers in the saloon, all of whom watched wide-eyed, then bowled through the batwings. With a quick glance over their shoulders they raced to their horses, mounted up, and galloped out of town.

Panting hard, Ned Bauer reached the marshal's office just as Zack Traynor was returning. Traynor was standing at the door and was about to enter when Bauer drew up and gasped, "Marshal! Trouble at the Bighorn! Those buffalo hunters who beat up Red Wolf the other day are back, and they're making mincemeat out of Earl Vine and Jerrold Kohler!"

Zack Traynor swore and started running toward the Bighorn Saloon with Ned Bauer at his heels. "Those dirty skunks don't listen to orders, obviously! They were told to get out of the county and stay out!" puffed Traynor as they ran.

When they reached the saloon, they learned that the ruffians had already left town, heading west. Traynor swore again and entered the Bighorn to see how badly Vine and Kohler had been beaten. Kohler was sitting up at a table, holding a wet cloth to his battered face, but Earl Vine lay flat on the floor, a puddle of water around his head. The bartender explained that he had poured the water on Vine's face, trying to revive him, but he was still out. Kneeling beside the fallen man, the marshal saw that blood was oozing from his skull.

Traynor swore a third time, then commanded, "Somebody go get Doc Sibley! Fast!"

When Sheridan's middle-aged physician burst through the batwings in less than five minutes, carrying his black bag, Zack Traynor was still kneeling beside the unconscious man. Sibley knelt on the man's other side and examined the gash, then thumbed Vine's eyelids back. Shaking his head, he asked, "Do I understand correctly? The same men did this who beat up Red Wolf?"

"That's correct, Doc," spoke up Ned Bauer, who stood near, watching with concern.

Sibley was quiet while he pulled a stethoscope from his bag, then listened to Vine's heartbeat. After a long moment, he placed the instrument back in the bag and said, "Zack, you'd better saddle up a posse. You'll be wanting those buffalo hunters for murder."

Traynor's brow furrowed, and he stared at the physician. "But Earl's not dead, Doc."

"He will be quite shortly," came Ben Sibley's reply. "They've cracked his skull. His brain's damaged. There's no way—"

At that instant a rattle sounded in Earl Vine's throat, and then his chest fell still. Sibley immediately laid his fingers to the side of Vine's neck. Rising to his feet, he sighed, pushed his hat to the back of his head, and pronounced solemnly, "Murder's the charge, Zack. Go get 'em."

Knowing that the killers already had a good start and not wanting to lose any more time forming a posse, Zack Traynor decided he would follow them alone and bring them in by himself. Moments later, he galloped out of Sheridan, heading westward. He found that the trail of the buffalo hunters was easy to follow: They were heading directly into the Bighorns.

Veronica Simmons had been at the Hardin cabin for nearly two hours when Meadowlark said, "Well, dear, it's time to cook up the noon meal." She laughed, adding, "Obadiah will be in here at twelve o'clock sharp with his stomach growling. He will say that repairing the barn door has given him a great appetite."

The young blonde chuckled. "Well, then, we certainly can't have him take a break from his labors and have nothing to feed him, can we?"

Putting down the rug they had been working on, the two women—looking like the living embodiments of night and day—made their way to the kitchen area. Veronica built a fire in the cookstove while Meadowlark began peeling potatoes. Every so often Veronica glanced over at

Red Wolf, who lay on a couch near the fireplace and watched them with tired eyes. The schoolteacher knew the aged Indian was steadily recovering from his beating, but it was a slow process, as his strength was not quick to return.

When Veronica had the fire going, she closed up the opening, then set two pans of water on top of the stove to heat. One was for boiling potatoes and the other was for washing dishes later. Looking over at the old Blackfoot, she called across the room, "Red Wolf, do you want to eat over there, or will you feel like sitting at the table with us?"

Red Wolf gave her a weak smile and replied, "I will eat with the rest of you, Veronica. Looking at your lovely face will put strength back into this old body."

Blushing slightly, although smiling at the compliment, Veronica began setting plates and eating utensils on the large trestle table. While she worked, her eyes strayed to the stuffed cougar head above the fireplace and, hanging just beneath it, the .50-caliber Sharps buffalo gun that had killed the beast. Veronica stared at the wild eyes and protruding fangs of the cougar for a moment, thinking of the scars that Will Hardin would wear on his face for the rest of his life. She then eyed the big rifle again and remarked to Meadowlark, "That gun that Will used to kill the cat, it looks as though it was just cleaned."

Meadowlark followed her guest's gaze, then agreed, "Oh, yes. My husband is very careful that his guns are regularly cleaned, work perfectly, and are loaded. His philosophy is that an unoiled, unloaded gun is no better than no gun at all."

"That makes sense," Veronica said with a little shrug.

"Everything Obadiah says always makes sense," Meadowlark remarked, her voice filled with love and respect for her husband.

The two women smiled at each other, then focused once again on the meal they were preparing.

Standing on a ladder that leaned against the barn be-

hind the house, Obadiah Hardin was fixing the top hinge
on the barn door. Sweat ran down his face, but although
the summer air was warm, Obadiah knew it was much
cooler up there in the Bighorns than it was down in
Sheridan, and he was grateful that he did not live in
town—for more reasons than the summer heat.

The mountain man stopped what he was doing for a
moment and reveled in the glorious day. A gentle breeze
was blowing, and Obadiah loved the music that it made in
the tall pines surrounding his place. That and the chatter-
ing of the animals and birds were generally the only sounds
the mountain dwellers heard, and Obadiah was thankful
that he did not have to listen to the noises of civilization.
With a sigh of pleasure he returned to his chore, inserting
a new screw in one of the holes in the hinge.

The nickering of a horse met his ears, and he could tell
it was not coming from his own animals in the corral or
from Veronica's horse, which was penned up with them.
The sound came from behind him in the yard.

After tightening the screw in place, the big man looked
over his shoulder. A stab of cold fear shot across his chest
as he saw the four scraggly riders heading his way, for he
recognized the brutal buffalo hunters immediately from
the description given him by Red Wolf. Obadiah knew
instantly that their appearance on his property signaled
that they were up to no good.

Shoving the screwdriver into his pocket, the mountain
man descended the ladder, cursing the fact that he was
unarmed. His feet had no sooner touched the ground
when the buffalo hunters pulled their guns on him. Their
act infuriated Obadiah Hardin. This was his property, and
they had no right trespassing on it, much less to hold him
at gunpoint.

As they were dismounting, he asked curtly, "What do
you want?"

Gordo Silcox, who was considerably larger than even
Hardin, sneered as he stepped close. "It ain't *what* we
want, pal. It's *who* we want."

"And who's that?"

"Well, I take it your name's Hardin—so that makes it your son we're lookin' for. Where is he?"

Glaring at the intruder, Obadiah Hardin snapped, "Will isn't here."

George Lang stepped beside his cohort, holding his revolver trained on Obadiah's chest, and blurted, "You're lyin'! He's here, all right."

"I'm not lying!" Obadiah countered. "And you'd better be glad of it. If Will *were* here, by now you'd be disarmed or dead. Best thing for you to do is get back on your horses and disappear."

"Tough talk for a man who's lookin' down the barrels of four guns, Hardin," Gordo Silcox snorted. "I say we go in the cabin, 'cause I think maybe we'll find our man in there."

Gesturing with the revolver, Silcox forced Obadiah to lead the way. As they neared the porch, the huge buffalo hunter ordered, "George, you go in first and get the drop on the lawman."

Without a word Lang charged into the cabin, waving his gun.

Meadowlark was facing toward the door when the tall, thin man came dashing in. Startled, she asked in a fearful voice, "Who are you? What—"

Veronica was at the stove, dropping potato slices into one of the pans of water, while on another burner a skillet sizzled with venison. She whirled around at the sound of Meadowlark's alarmed words just as Obadiah came through the door with his hands up, followed by the other miscreants.

George Lang looked past the stunned Indian woman to Veronica. Laughing, he said, "You must be the deputy's sweetie. Right, beautiful? Lookee here, Gordo! Mmm-mmm! Ain't she somethin'?"

Ignoring Lang's question, Gordo Silcox looked carefully around the large room, glared at Red Wolf lying on the couch, then demanded of Meadowlark, "Where's Cougar?"

"He's on duty in town," she answered coldly.

Swinging his gun on her, the giant snarled, "You're lyin', woman! Now, you tell me where he is, or you get a bullet between the eyes!"

"She's telling you the truth!" Obadiah shouted. "I told you the truth, too! Will isn't here!"

Mel Goss stepped in front of Obadiah and stuck his gun on the tip of the big man's nose. Eyes wild, Goss hissed, "The man at the general store told me your kid was spendin' time right here, today. With his girlfriend, Veronica." Throwing a glance at the blonde, he asked, "You're Veronica, ain't you?"

Veronica's face was stiff with fear. Nodding, she whispered hoarsely, "Yes."

Looking back at Obadiah, Goss blared, "So where's Cougar?"

Terrified for Obadiah's life, Veronica spoke up. "Will is on an errand in Bingham right now."

"Bingham?" Goss echoed, still holding the muzzle of his gun against Obadiah's nose. "Why, that's more than twenty miles from here." Staring coldly at the young woman, Goss asked, "So he's comin' here from there, is that it?"

Obadiah answered, "We don't know when he'll be through in Bingham. There's no way to—"

"Shut up!" bellowed Goss, shoving the muzzle hard into Obadiah's skin. "I'm talkin' to Veronica!" Looking back at the blonde, he said, "Okay, girl, give me the story. And you'd better tell me the truth, or I'm shootin' Hardin's nose off!"

Veronica's hands began to shake, and it was obvious that she was having trouble talking. Finally choking out the words, she said, "Will . . . Will is to be here late in the afternoon. Just before suppertime."

Goss looked to Gordo Silcox. The huge man rubbed his fleshy chin and grunted, "I think she's tellin' the truth. So we'll just have to wait here till he shows up." He snorted, adding, "We owe that scar-faced dude plenty . . . and this is one time we're payin' our debts."

Silcox waved his gun at the mountain man and, pointing with his chin toward a chair, ordered, "Sit down, Hardin. And don't give me no trouble or these women get it."

Obadiah scowled at him but obeyed.

Silcox then ordered his cohort, "George, go outside and hide our horses. We don't want Cougar seein' 'em when he rides in, 'cause we want to keep this little homecomin' party a surprise. We'll leave our rifles on the porch and ambush him just before he rides into the yard."

Veronica gasped, and Obadiah looked over at her. The young woman's hand was at her mouth, and the blood had drained from her face, leaving it almost colorless. Glancing at his wife, he could tell that Meadowlark was experiencing the same terror. A cold knot formed in the mountain man's stomach, for he had no doubt that these dastardly men would gun down his unsuspecting son when Will Hardin rode in for supper.

Obadiah's mind began racing. He knew he had to do something . . . but what? These men were vicious and determined—and by their very actions it was clear that they had committed murder before.

He remembered his Remington repeater rifle stuck behind the tall cabinet near the door. Looking casually in that direction, he could see the dark wood of the rifle butt barely exposed at the edge of the cabinet. The weapon was fully loaded and there was a cartridge in the chamber, and if he could get his hands on it, all he had to do was cock the hammer and start shooting. But it was a mighty big "if," and the trick would be to get his hands on it without taking a few slugs in the process.

George Lang strode toward the door in response to Silcox's order. Looking over his shoulder, he winked at Veronica and told her in an insinuating voice, "I'll be back, good-lookin'."

Obadiah saw red. Baring his teeth, he snapped, "You leave her alone!"

Lang merely laughed and stepped outside.

Silcox then told Goss, "Mel, station yourself on the

porch and keep your eyes peeled, just in case our young friend shows up early." He then ordered his son, "Jonathan, keep your eye on that old redskin." The giant suddenly guffawed, adding, "Though from the looks of him, after that beatin' we gave him, he ain't gonna cause much trouble." He then breathed deeply and said mockingly, "These nice ladies were right nice to be fixin' us a meal— and my nose tells me it's venison. Mel, we'll bring your food out to you."

"Okay, Gordo," Goss quickly responded, then hurried outside to the porch and dragged a straight-backed chair over to where he could best watch the trail.

Jonathan Silcox shuffled over to the couch where Red Wolf lay and, the revolver in his hand held casually, stood watching him.

Holding his own pistol near Obadiah's head, the gang leader commanded Veronica and Meadowlark, "Dish out that food, ladies. As soon as George gets back, we're gonna eat."

"But the food is not quite ready," protested the Indian woman. "You will have to wait."

"Well, then, hurry it up!" Silcox barked.

Jumping at the man's words, Meadowlark joined Veronica at the stove and helped with the cooking. Obadiah watched the women solicitously and noticed the schoolteacher glancing at the pan of water that would soon be boiling. She and Meadowlark then flashed eye signals between them, and the mountain man knew that they, too, felt something must be done before Will Hardin arrived. The young lawman would not stand a chance if he was ambushed.

George Lang returned and sauntered close to the kitchen area, looking at Veronica with hungry eyes. Obadiah read his intent and warned, "You stay away from her, mister."

Lang pointed his revolver at Obadiah and sneered, retorting, "And just what are you gonna do about it, big man?"

Obadiah could only glare at his challenger, wishing he

could put his hands around Lang's neck and slowly strangle him.

"Stay out of her way and let her finish with that food," Gordo Silcox told his partner, who reluctantly did as he was told.

Veronica sidestepped Lang and began dishing out the food with Meadowlark. The women and Obadiah surreptitiously glanced at each other, passing silent agreement that when one of them found the opportunity to make a move, the others would respond at the same moment.

The food was finally served to the captors, and the men ate with gusto. Suddenly Mel Goss hurried in from his post out on the porch and shouted, "A rider's comin' up the trail! Gordo, there's a rider comin'!"

Veronica's head whipped around, and her face was as white as a sheet when she looked at Obadiah, who was feeling the same agony the young woman was clearly experiencing. Cougar was arriving ahead of time—and they had no way of stopping him from riding into the trap.

Leaving Jonathan Silcox and Mel Goss to hold guns on their prisoners, Gordo Silcox took George Lang and bolted for the door. Grabbing their rifles, the buffalo hunters dashed to the trees that lined the trail. After a few seconds, they saw the sun reflect off the badge on the rider's chest. "It's him, Gordo!" exclaimed Lang in a hoarse whisper.

The gang leader started to agree, then studied the shape of the man in the saddle. "No, it ain't," he breathed, his voice disappointed. "It's the marshal. What's he doin' here?"

Lang scratched his filthy hair, his face screwed up in puzzlement. "Dunno, but he's here. What're we gonna do?"

"Kill him. Come on. Let's move a little farther from the cabin."

Rushing through the trees, the killers found a good spot and positioned themselves. Guns ready, they waited for Zack Traynor to ride into their sights, and moments later he appeared, studying the tracks on the ground.

Silcox lined his rifle on Traynor and whispered to his cohort, "Okay, George. Me first. As soon as I fire, give him another one."

Lang's rodentlike face gleamed with anticipated pleasure as he caressed the rifle with his left hand while curling his right forefinger over the trigger. Suddenly the giant's rifle boomed, and Lang fired a second later, grinning demonically. When Marshal Zack Traynor peeled out of the saddle, the feral-looking man giggled like a small child.

Gordo Silcox stepped out from behind the tree and managed to corral the lawman's fleeing horse as it hurried toward him. Looking at the fallen form lying in a heap farther down the trail, Silcox shouldered his rifle and quipped, "Well, so much for the marshal. Come on. Let's go dump the body into that gully just over yonder and put this animal in the barn—after all, we don't want nothin' signalin' Cougar that somethin's wrong—and then we can finish that venison." Chuckling, he remarked, "I gotta hand it to Cougar. He sure knows how to pick a woman. She cooks as good as she looks." He suddenly began to laugh. "Hey! I made a poem! Pretty good, huh?" Then his grin faded. "And speakin' of the blonde, don't forget to keep your mind on what we came for . . . so keep your hands off her, George. Got it?"

Lang looked glumly at the giant. "Yeah. I got it."

"Good. I wouldn't want to see nothin' happen to *you*."

Chapter Six

When the rifle shots echoed across the mountain, Veronica Simmons began trembling uncontrollably while cold sweat dampened her brow. She looked over at Obadiah Hardin, who had closed his eyes and gritted his teeth, and at Meadowlark Hardin, who was biting down hard on a finger, her face twisted with agony. Tearing her gaze away from her beloved's parents, the schoolteacher looked toward the open doorway and whispered Will Hardin's name.

Jonathan Silcox suddenly chuckled. When Veronica caught his vacant glance, he remarked, "Sounds like Pa and George took care of that deputy. Serves him right for beatin' us and throwin' us in jail."

Scowling at the dullard, Veronica opened her mouth to say something, but he flicked the revolver that he held on Obadiah menacingly close to the mountain man's ear and she held her tongue.

The young woman abruptly started toward the door, but Mel Goss jumped in her path and rasped, "No, you don't, lady! Get back over there by the stove. You'll get to see your sweetie's body shortly—as soon as Gordo and George bring him."

The wait was torturous for the captives. A quarter hour had passed before the two killers finally appeared, stepping heavily onto the porch, then moving inside the cabin.

The eager look on Jonathan's face died as he hurried to the doorway and looked around outside. "Where's Cougar's body, Pa?" he asked in a disappointed voice.

Meadowlark and Veronica gripped each other's hands, their eyes fixed on Silcox and Lang, while Red Wolf sat on the couch unmoving and Obadiah held his breath.

"It wasn't Cougar we killed, son," Silcox replied. "It was that marshal . . . what's his name? Traynor." His face was thoughtful for a moment, then he muttered, "I keep wonderin' what he was doin' up here."

The prisoners released a collective sigh of immense relief, though Veronica was saddened and sickened by Zack Traynor's murder and her friends clearly felt the same way.

Silcox sent Mel Goss back to the porch to watch the trail, then sat down at the table to finish his meal. George Lang moved across the room toward Veronica, his eyes fixed on the young schoolmarm. Grinning evilly, Lang drew close to Veronica and said, "Before I eat, I'm gonna get me a nice kiss from this beauty."

Obadiah's face went beet red. Ignoring the muzzle of Jonathan Silcox's revolver, he leapt up from his chair and shouted, "You stay away from her!"

Lang started to reply, but Silcox interrupted in a cold voice, "George, I told you, now ain't the time for that kind of stuff. Eat your meal so's we can be ready for Cougar when he comes. Remember what I said: I want your mind on what we're here for." He then glared at the mountain man and ordered, "And you, Hardin, siddown!"

Reluctantly Lang moved away from Veronica to eat his food as Obadiah sank into the chair.

Hearing the bubbling sound of the now-boiling water on the stove, Veronica suddenly got an idea. It meant luring the repulsive George Lang close to her, but it was their only hope. Her heart pounding, she waited for the right moment.

Silcox and Lang sat down and began eating noisily. The giant informed his brother and Goss that the marshal's body had been dumped in a ravine and his horse put in the barn. Cougar would still ride up to the cabin thinking all was well—and soon he would be as dead as his boss.

While the men were preoccupied with congratulating each other on their plan, Veronica glanced furtively at Meadowlark, nodding almost imperceptively toward George Lang, then at the pot of water. The Indian woman nodded back, indicating that she understood.

The young woman stayed close to the stove in spite of the heat, waiting for Lang to look her way again. He finally did when he was almost finished eating, and when their eyes met, Veronica gave him a small, coquettish smile. The man's eyes lit up. Hurriedly, he gorged down the last of his food and looked toward his leader, who was busy licking his plate.

With the pot hidden behind her body, Veronica managed to feel for the handle of the pot and turn it to be ready to fling it at Lang. Catching Obadiah's eyes, she gave him a covert look, flicked her eyes briefly at Lang, then again caught the mountain man's eye. He looked slightly puzzled for a moment, then nodded that he understood. At the same time, his body stiffened as he braced himself, clearly ready to make a move.

Lang got up from the table, all the while watching Silcox from the corner of his eye, and inched his way toward Veronica. Quickly Obadiah shifted his body, slightly blocking Veronica from Silcox's view, and started talking to the giant, distracting him. "What do you plan to do with us once you've killed my son?" he asked.

Gordo Silcox replied that he had not decided yet. He snickered, adding, "You'll learn soon enough. Don't worry."

As George Lang sidled toward Veronica, Meadowlark stepped aside, giving him room. The young blonde gave him another smile, and when Lang was four feet from her, she told him softly, "I've got something special for you."

Obviously believing Veronica was finally receptive to his advances, Lang grinned and asked, "Oh, yeah? And what's that?"

Veronica turned very slowly so as not to alarm him, keeping the pan from his sight. Gripping the handle with both hands, she turned back around smoothly and said, "This!" As she spoke, she flung the steaming water squarely into his face.

Lang screamed in agony, throwing his hands to his scalded face. He staggered about blindly, finally smashing against the cupboard and falling to his knees.

With the other intruders' attention drawn to their cohort, Obadiah reached up and grabbed Jonathan Silcox's shirt, hurling him toward the kitchen area. Taken completely by surprise, the huge, slow-minded ruffian tumbled into the big table and crashed to the floor. Brandishing the pan as a makeshift weapon, Veronica flung it at Jonathan, bouncing it off his head.

With the young man temporarily removed as an obstacle, Obadiah dived past a surprised Gordo Silcox toward the cabinet by the door. Veronica looked wildly around, searching for something else to use as a weapon, while Meadowlark raced to the drawer where the utensils were kept and palmed a large butcher knife.

Abruptly Mel Goss came charging in through the doorway, his revolver cocked. His gaze falling first on the Indian woman, he cursed loudly at her, then pointed his revolver at her and fired, hitting Meadowlark in the chest and killing her instantly. Veronica screamed, almost unable to believe her eyes. Shaking herself from the horror that gripped her, she lunged for the fallen knife, but Jonathan had gained his feet and was lumbering toward the blonde, his ordinarily dull eyes blazing.

Gritting her teeth, Veronica swung the butcher knife at the enormous young man as he came at her with murder in his eyes. The blade ripped along his sleeve, biting into his flesh, but the powerful youth easily knocked the knife from her hand and seized her and threw her violently across the room. She slammed into a small table near the fireplace, twisting her right leg as she landed and cracking her head against the wall. The table broke from the impact, sending the lantern that sat on it to the floor with a crash, spilling kerosene all over. Veronica collapsed in a half-conscious state.

Gordo Silcox had dropped his plate and now clawed for his gun. Bringing the weapon around, he aimed at Obadiah, who was racing across the room toward his hidden rifle, and shot the mountain man in the back. Obadiah stiffened, bowing his wide shoulders, and fell just short of the cabinet.

Rousing himself from the shock of seeing his daughter murdered, Red Wolf managed to stand and stumbled toward the Sharps buffalo rifle hanging above the fireplace. He had just grabbed it when Mel Goss turned his revolver on the old Blackfoot, firing twice. One bullet ricocheted off the stone fireplace, but the other ripped into the aged Indian's side. Red Wolf buckled and dropped the Sharps, but he did not go down. Seeing Gordo Silcox about to shoot Obadiah again, the old Blackfoot summoned all his strength and charged into the buffalo hunter just as he fired, spoiling his aim. Silcox howled at the old man, who managed to skitter out of his way.

Obadiah, on his belly, grabbed his rifle and slowly brought it to bear on the giant, but from the corner of his eye he saw Mel Goss bringing his gun around to shoot him, and Obadiah fired first. The slug ripped into Goss's heart, killing him instantly.

Shouting with anger, Jonathan Silcox picked up his fallen revolver and brought it to bear on Obadiah Hardin just as the mountain man struggled to his feet. Obadiah tried to bring the rifle up, but Jonathan fired before he could do so, hitting him in the chest. Obadiah staggered and again tried vainly to raise the rifle, but the huge youth snarled, "That wasn't enough for you, huh?" and shot him a second time, though his aim was off and the bullet hit more to the side.

Wincing with pain, Jonathan looked at his bleeding arm, then swore vociferously, taking his attention from Obadiah. Although the big mountain man was bleeding profusely, he was was still able to stand, and he lurched toward the dim-witted young buffalo hunter. Obadiah Hardin grabbed him with his powerful arms, and the gun slipped from Jonathan's hand and clattered to the floor. In spite of his wounds, Obadiah locked his wrist in his hand behind Jonathan's back and squeezed with all his might. It was as though the youth were being crushed by a vise. Howling with pain, he called for his father to help him before he was squeezed to death.

Hearing his son's cry, Silcox ceased his violent assault on Red Wolf, who lay bleeding on the floor. Swearing at him, the giant leaned down and clubbed the old man solidly on the head with his revolver, cracking his skull. He then dashed to his son's aid.

Jonathan's spine was about to snap from the pressure of Obadiah's mighty arms when Silcox stepped up behind the mountain man and slammed the barrel of his pistol against Obadiah's head again and again until he collapsed.

From where she lay with her leg twisted beneath her, Veronica finally shook off her torpor. Seeing the assault on Obadiah, she screamed at Silcox to stop beating him. "Please! Leave him alone!" she begged, tears coursing down her pale cheeks.

Ignoring her, Gordo Silcox looked at his son, who was leaning against the nearest wall, gasping for breath and holding his blood-soaked sleeve. "Are you all right?" Silcox asked.

"I . . . I think so, Pa." He then scowled at Veronica. "That . . . that woman cut me. I'm gonna kill her!"

"Oh, no, you ain't!"

Both Hardins turned at the sound of George Lang's strangled voice coming from behind them. Lang's face was blistered and raw, but he was able to see. Walking stiffly toward Veronica, he hissed, "*I'm* the one who's gonna kill her!"

"Neither of you ain't!" blared Gordo Silcox. "We're gettin' outta here, and she's goin' with us. Her boyfriend is bound to track us, and we'll need her as a hostage. With her in our hands, we'll have an edge on him." He looked the beautiful young woman up and down as though suddenly seeing her for the first time, then added, "Besides. I've a mind to keep her for myself."

"Why can't we just take our stand right here, Pa?" whined Jonathan. "We can ambush him just like we did the marshal."

"No," Silcox replied, shaking his head forcefully. "This place is real bad luck. Besides, we need to recover some. Mel's dead, you're cut up bad, and George is burned somethin' terrible. We'll get outta here and find someplace to hole up in. Remember how the deputy took on the lot of us before? And there was *four* of us then, and we was all in one piece! No. We'll stand a better chance later on somewhere else."

Looking closely at Lang, Silcox winced, then muttered, "Let's see if we can find some stuff for them blisters, George."

The giant rifled through the cupboards and found some salve that Meadowlark had labeled for burns. He handed the jar to Lang, then gestured at the dead woman, saying, "I'll give them Indians this much: They usually know what they're talkin' about when it comes to medicinals. This stuff'll probably help some."

Lang applied the herbal preparation to his blistered skin, then exclaimed, "Hey, you're right, Gordo! My face don't hurt nearly so much no more!"

"Good. Then you can help me see to the horses—and saddle one up for the blonde."

Jonathan was left to guard Veronica, and despite her pain, the young brute forced her to bandage his arm. She reluctantly obeyed, avoiding his hate-filled eyes. When she was finished, he scowled at her, promising, "Somehow I'm gonna convince my pa that he don't need you. And when I do, I'm gonna tear you into pieces!"

Fear prickled Veronica's skin, for she knew the evil young man meant what he was saying. *Oh, Will,* she thought, *you've got to save me from these beasts!*

Silcox and George came through the door and picked up Mel Goss's body. They took it outside, carried it down to where they had tossed Zack Traynor's body, and heaved it into the ravine. When they returned, the giant grabbed Veronica by the wrist and jerked her off the couch, saying acidly, "Come on, girl. Time to ride."

Veronica fell to the floor with a whimper. "I can't ride. It's my knee. Something's badly torn up."

Silcox gathered her up in his arms and growled, "It don't matter none, 'cause you're goin' with us!" As he carried her toward the door, the terrified young woman gazed sadly at the unmoving bodies of Meadowlark, Obadiah, and Red Wolf. Saying silent prayers for them, she began to weep. As Silcox stepped through the doorway, she was still looking back, knowing it would be the last time she would ever see her friends. When Will Hardin returned home, he would immediately bury his family. More tears sprang to her eyes as she thought of the pain her beloved would experience, and she wished she could be there to try to comfort him.

Setting Veronica roughly down, Silcox told his son, "Go get your horse, Jonathan. I'll join you in a minute."

Jonathan gestured back inside at Obadiah, who lay unconscious on the floor, barely breathing, and said, "The old man's still alive, Pa. Let me kill him."

"I told you to go get your horse!" barked Silcox. "Now, do it!"

The youth stomped past Veronica, who quickly turned her head and looked back into the cabin, her heart beating fast. Obadiah was still alive! She watched Silcox check first Red Wolf then Meadowlark, making certain they were dead. Satisfied, he stood over the mountain man, smiling wickedly. "Two in the chest and one in the back," he said, a note of admiration in his voice. "Well, you're not long for this world, Hardin, but the question is: Should I finish you off, or let you die slow?" Chuckling, he turned away, saying, "Yeah. Go ahead and die slow."

Veronica hurriedly looked away as Gordo Silcox stepped

back onto the porch. Bending, he swooped her up in his powerful arms and started toward the barn.

Stirring, moaning softly, Obadiah Hardin fought his way back to consciousness. He was vaguely aware that the buffalo hunters were preparing to leave, and calling upon every ounce of energy left in his body, he rolled to his knees. He could hear Gordo Silcox talking roughly to Veronica, telling her she had to ride, no matter how much pain she was experiencing.

With tremendous effort Obadiah crawled to the kitchen table and groped his way to his feet, then staggered toward his rifle and picked it up. Jacking a cartridge into the chamber, he staggered toward the door. When he reached it, he rested against the frame, blinking to focus his vision. The killers were already heading out of the yard toward the trail and were not looking back. Gordo Silcox was riding in front, leading Veronica Simmons's horse. Behind Veronica was George Lang, and Jonathan Silcox was bringing up the rear.

Hardin stumbled onto the porch and leaned against a post. Shouldering the rifle, he sighted in on Jonathan's broad back and squeezed the trigger. The weapon bucked in his hands as it roared, and Jonathan took the bullet in his left shoulder, slumping forward in the saddle.

Obadiah's head began to spin, and he dropped the rifle and clung to the post that held up the porch roof. Hearing Gordo Silcox swear loudly, he looked down the trail to see Silcox pulling his gun. Although he knew he should move out of harm's way, he could not summon the ability to do so.

The giant fired twice, but the first bullet missed, chewing into the log wall near the door. The second hit Obadiah in the abdomen, buckling him. Groaning, the mountain man toppled from the porch and sprawled faceup on the ground.

Cursing himself for not finishing Hardin off before he had left the cabin, Gordo Silcox stared at the inert figure of Obadiah Hardin and growled, "He's dead. Come on. Let's ride."

*   *   *

Obadiah Hardin opened his eyes to see the treetops above him swirling against the blue Wyoming sky. With his strength completely gone, he could not move, and he no longer felt any pain. All he could feel was the blood slowly seeping from his wounds, dampening the earth beneath him.

Lying there with four bullets sucking the life from his body, Obadiah refused to die. He willed himself to stay alive until his son arrived. *Will must know what happened,* he thought. *He must know what happened, who did it, and that the vicious killers have Veronica.* His mind strayed to Meadowlark and her father lying dead in the cabin, and tears flooded his eyes.

The sun was sinking low when Cougar Will Hardin trotted his mount up the trail. The cabin soon came into view, but the moment he saw it, he knew something was wrong. Supper should be on the stove, but there was no smoke coming from the chimney. Tiny needles of fear stabbed his spine as he spurred the horse up the steep slope. Seconds later he swung into the yard and saw his father lying on the ground in front of the cabin. His heart froze in his breast and his forehead went clammy with sweat as he sent his horse into a fast canter.

Reining to a quick stop, he vaulted from the saddle. "Pa!" he gasped, kneeling beside Obadiah.

The mountain man's eyes were glassy, and Cougar could see that he was clinging to life by a thread. Obadiah was lying in a pool of blood and his shirt was soaked with the shiny crimson fluid.

"Pa, what happened?" Cougar asked, his voice catching and his body rigid. He shot a glance toward the cabin, thinking of Meadowlark, Red Wolf, and Veronica.

Obadiah licked his lips, and his voice came out in a squeaky rasp as he said with pained effort, "It . . . was those . . . those buffalo hunters, son. Silcox." He coughed, and there was a strange sound in his lungs. Finally he continued, "They killed . . . your mother and . . . Grandpa. Took . . . took Veronica with . . . them."

Cougar felt his body first go hot, then cold. Grief mingled with rage churned within him. "Pa," he said softly, "let me take you inside. I'll get the bleeding stopped and ride for Doc Sibley. Then me and Zack'll go after those scum."

Obadiah shook his head slowly. "No time," he gasped. "They also killed . . . Zack."

The young deputy suddenly felt completely alone. "Zack? They killed Zack, too?"

"Yeah. Ambushed him. I . . . I don't know why . . . he came here, but they . . . cut him down on the trail. They . . . were planning on ambushing . . . you. Said they threw . . . his body into the . . . ravine. I . . . killed the one called Goss. Shot Silcox's son as they . . . they were riding away. Don't know if I . . . killed him."

Will Hardin went numb all over, and he felt as though he had fallen into some terrible nightmare from which he could not awaken. "Pa, I'm going to carry you inside," he said, running his arms under the heavy, muscular frame. Standing with his burden, he cradled his father gently in his arms, holding him as he would carry a child.

The mountain man groaned, then coughed and spit blood. Looking into his son's eyes, he whispered, "Get 'em, son. Make 'em pay. And . . . don't let 'em hurt Veronica. She . . . she's in love with you. She—"

Obadiah Hardin's eyes rolled back into their sockets, and his body went limp. Cougar knew he was gone. He looked into his father's slack, lifeless face, and the pain and loss he felt went all the way through to his bones. Suddenly a primitive animal cry of sheer torment echoed across the mountains as Will Hardin gave vent to the anguish that tore at his soul.

The young man wept as he carried Obadiah's body to the porch, then entered the cabin. When he looked upon the corpses of Meadowlark and Red Wolf, he cried again, releasing his almost torturous grief.

Moving like a man in a trance, Will Hardin carried the bodies to a small open plot at the rear of the cabin. While tears scalded his cheeks, he dug three graves, completing them by lantern light. Tenderly, he wrapped the bodies in blankets and lowered them into the hard earth. When he had filled in the graves, he returned to the cabin and took Meadowlark's Bible from her dresser, then walked in measured steps back outside.

Setting down the lantern, he stood over the graves, and the lamp cast flickering shadows on the newly turned ground. Holding the Bible so that he could read by the lamplight, he began in a quivering voice, " 'I am the resurrection, and the life: He that believeth in me, though he were dead, yet shall he live.' " Thumbing further with shaky fingers, he found another place so well taught him by his stepmother. The night breeze plucked at the pages as he found the correct spot and again read aloud. " 'So when this corruptible shall have put on incorruption, and this mortal shall have put on immortality, then shall be brought to pass the saying that is written, Death is swallowed up in victory. O death, where is thy sting? O grave, where is thy victory?' "

He choked out the last few words as he clutched Meadowlark's Bible to his chest and fought the lump in his throat. When his voice was free again, he recited from memory, " 'The Lord giveth, and the Lord taketh away. Blessed be the name of the Lord.' " The wind whistling through the tall pines—the music his father had so dearly loved—was the only sound as Cougar stood silently staring at the three graves for a long moment.

He then picked up the lantern and headed back toward the cabin. As he walked he said, "Lord, it seems to me that You didn't take them away . . . those killers did. You gave them to me, but Silcox and his fiendish bunch took them away. I know it says in this book that vengeance is Yours, that You will repay. But this time I'm going to help You out on that score—and I sure do hope You will help me in turn."

The young lawman took the lantern down the trail a piece and, after searching for a while, spotted Marshal Zack Traynor's body some fifteen feet down in the shallow ravine where the murderers had dumped it. Thirty minutes later Will Hardin headed back to Sheridan in the moonlight, leading Zack Traynor's horse with the body of the marshal draped over the saddle.

Tears scalded Hardin's cheeks as he thought of the brave but useless fight his family had waged. Obadiah had taken care of at least one of the buffalo hunters; he would take care of the others. His teeth clenched, the deputy vowed, "If any of those scum harm Ronnie, they'll wish they'd never been born."

Suddenly he recalled what his father had said with his dying breath: "Don't let 'em hurt Veronica. She's in love with you."

Those last five words seemed to seep into Cougar's brain as slowly as molasses pours in winter. He turned them repeatedly over in his mind. Abruptly, like dawn breaking on a new day, Will Hardin saw the light. Veronica Simmons did not merely love him as a friend loves another friend, she was *in* love with him. Memories of times spent with her over the years came flooding through his mind, and words she had dropped here and there indicated clearly that she was in love with him without her actually coming out and saying it. He recalled countless tender acts of love on her part that he had taken— *mis*taken—as deeds of mere friendship.

Suddenly thwacking his forehead, the deputy scolded himself aloud. "Will Hardin, you utter, blind fool! You're in love with her, too! The two of us have been in love since who knows when, but she thinks it's only one-sided. And no wonder. You were too blind to see it, too wrapped up in other things to recognize what was going on in your own heart. How could you have been so slow to recognize the truth? And why did you have to be so thickheaded that it took a tragedy like this to wake you up? She's the only one you have in the world now—and you'd better find her before you lose her, too!"

An icy feeling settled over Hardin as he realized that if the brutes who had her should kill Veronica, she would die without ever having heard him say he was in love with her.

Cougar's steel-gray eyes hardened as he reached the bottom of the mountain, seeing the lights of Sheridan twinkling in the distance. Rage burned within him toward the men who dared take the lives of his family and take sweet Veronica as their hostage. He fought to shake from his mind what such despicable men might do to her.

"Oh, God," he said, shuddering, "please spare Ronnie that we might have our lives together."

Chapter Seven

Arriving in Sheridan just past nine-thirty at night, Will Hardin brought Zack Traynor's body to the undertaking parlor, solemnly removing the badge from the dead man's chest. He then went around from house to house, gathering the councilmen and other prominent citizens of the town. Assembling them in front of the marshal's office, the young deputy told them what had happened at the Hardin cabin and that he was going after the buffalo hunters. "Someone will have to take charge of law enforcement while I'm gone," he told the large crowd.

Ralph Coe, council chairman, spoke up. "Will, I say let's form a posse so we can rescue Veronica Simmons and bring those killers in for hanging."

Shaking his head slowly, Cougar responded, "I'm afraid if Silcox and his bunch see a posse on their trail, they might kill Veronica. You never know how madmen might react. It's better if I go alone. I'll find them, and I'll figure out a way somehow to get the drop on them."

There was a murmuring in the crowd, then Hardin continued, "As I was saying, Sheridan's going to need someone to take over the marshal's office to protect all you good folks while I'm gone—somebody who's good with a gun."

"We've got a few men to pick from," Coe suggested, "but I think the first thing we ought to do is make you our marshal. I don't think there's anyone among us who'd object to that."

There was immediate and unanimous agreement, and Will Hardin was sworn in as marshal of Sheridan on the spot, with the badge he had removed from Zack Traynor pinned on the young lawman's buckskin shirt. With that done, Hardin suggested that one of the men in the crowd, Dan Turner, a man slightly older than Cougar who had ridden on a few posses and who was good with firearms, be appointed deputy. Turner readily accepted, the town councilmen approved the selection, and Turner was also sworn in.

"I've got to ride to the Simmons place and tell Ronnie's folks what happened," the new marshal told his new deputy. "From there, I'll go back to my pa's place for the rest of the night, and at dawn I'll pick up the Silcox gang's trail and head out after them."

After giving Turner some additional instructions, Cougar went to his house and packed his saddlebags with plenty of ammunition and enough food for several days. From there he rode out to the Simmons ranch, arriving near midnight. As he rode into the yard he was not surprised to see lamplight streaming from the windows. The Simmonses were no doubt wondering why their daughter had not yet arrived home and were probably pacing the floor.

Hardin stepped onto the porch and knocked at the door. There were rapid footsteps, and the door was flung open. A harried-looking Letha Simmons gasped, "Oh, Will! Something's wrong! Veronica hasn't come home yet!"

"I know, ma'am," Cougar replied softly. "Is Mr. Simmons here?"

"No. He took one of our men and rode to your father's place. They've been gone awhile now." Suddenly her eyes narrowed in her worried face, and she said, "You *know* she's not home? How do you know that—and what do you know?"

Hardin would not withhold the truth from Veronica's mother, for she had a right to know the danger her daughter was facing. Quickly he told her the whole story, assuring her that he intended to ride the buffalo hunters down and rescue Veronica before she was harmed. Letha wept over the deaths of Obadiah, Meadowlark, and Red Wolf, then clung to the young lawman, tearfully pleading with him to bring her daughter home safely.

"I promise you, Mrs. Simmons, I'm going to do just that." So saying, Cougar rode away in the moonlight, heading for his old home.

Hardin was just beginning to weave up the winding trail that led to his father's cabin when he met Dale Simmons and his ranch hand coming down. The bright moonlight revealed that Simmons was almost in a state of panic, and when Cougar told him what had happened, the rancher looked as though he might faint from the shock. After recovering, Simmons said that he and his man had not seen the graves behind the house, but they had known something was wrong when they had not found anyone at home that late.

Turning to the ranch hand, Simmons said, "Jack, you ride on back home and tell Letha that I'm riding with Will. I'm going with him to help rescue Veronica."

"Mr. Simmons," Cougar put in, "I appreciate how worried you are about Ronnie, but it's really best if I do this alone."

The rancher shook his head forcefully. "She's my daughter, Will! I'm going with you!"

"Please, sir," Cougar responded, keeping his voice level, "those men are desperate and dangerous. It'll be much easier for one man to sneak up on them and catch them off guard. You know that I'm very experienced at this sort of thing, and believe me, I would only do what was best for Ronnie. Please trust me, sir. Her chances of being rescued will be much better if I ride alone."

Simmons scrubbed a nervous hand over his eyes and said with a tremor in his voice, "That's my little girl they've got, Will. Certainly you can understand my concern."

"Of course I can—even more than you know." He paused a moment, then added softly, "You see, sir, I've come to realize that I'm in love with your daughter."

Dale Simmons stared at the young lawman for a moment, then managed a small smile. "Life's ironic, isn't it? It's when we think we might lose something that we realize how valuable it is to us."

Hardin nodded slowly. "That's certainly the truth, Mr. Simmons. But I guarantee you I know it now."

Simmons put his hand on Hardin's shoulder. "I'm going to trust you with my little girl's life, Will. Since you say her chances are better if you go alone, I'll stay here." Tears filled his eyes. "Just bring her home safe and sound."

"I will, sir. I promise. I will."

At the first light of dawn, after a night of little sleep, Cougar Will Hardin rode off. He soon found the spot where Gordo Silcox and his men had left the trail and headed on a southerly angle out of the mountains.

Sunlight shafted through the tall, heavy timber, dappling the forest floor, as Sheridan's new marshal threaded his way down the steep slopes. Following the hoofprints of the horses that carried the murderers and their captive was easy. The men seemed to be making no effort to cover their trail.

As Cougar continued his downward trek, praying that he would find Veronica in time to spare her harm, he suddenly heard a deep canine growl, followed by angry, vicious barking and snapping teeth. Pulling rein, he listened, wondering if he was about to encounter a wolf. Then he heard a man's voice shouting a string of profanities, his tone one of annoyance.

Loosening the revolver in his holster, Hardin nudged

his horse forward, holding it to a walk. As he drew nearer the growling and cursing, the sounds grew louder in volume until, some fifty feet ahead through the trees, he caught sight of a balding, stocky man standing a few feet from a huge black dog that was snarling and snapping at him.

Slipping from the saddle, Hardin hurried through the timber. The man saw him as he drew near and abruptly stopped his cursing. Hardin saw that the dog had a foreleg caught in the steel jaws of a trap, which, by its size, he figured was a coyote trap. Several yards farther was the man's tent, and a horse and mule were lazily cropping grass nearby. The man was obviously a trapper who was cashing in on the bounty offered in towns all over northern Wyoming for coyote pelts.

"Caught me a dog, Marshal," said the trapper, noting the badge on Hardin's chest. "Though I guess you can see that. But the stupid critter won't let me free him from the trap. Ugly beast keeps snappin' at me."

Will Hardin eyed the dog. Its coat was thick and shaggy and as black as midnight. He could attach no particular breed to the animal but figured it weighed at least a hundred and fifty pounds. It was also the ugliest dog he had ever laid eyes on, and he thought the sight of it would put a chill down any man's spine. "He's obviously scared and in pain," remarked Hardin. "The teeth of that trap have cut his leg. You can see the blood. I'm sure your cursing at him only frightens him more."

"Yeah, but the stupid mutt oughtta know I'm tryin' to help him," countered the trapper. Moving in close again, he scowled at the dog and said angrily, "Now, if you hold still, mutt, you'll soon be out of the trap."

The dog crouched and bared its fangs, growling from deep within its chest.

The trapper swore and bellowed, "You dumb beast! I'm tryin' to help you!"

Pulling at the trap with its bleeding leg, the dog sprayed spittle as it snapped and slashed at the trapper.

The man leapt back and drew the revolver on his hip. "You mangy cur!" he railed, thumbing back the hammer. "I'll kill you!"

"Hold it!" blared Cougar, lunging in and grabbing the man's wrist, thrusting it upward. The revolver discharged, sending the bullet harmlessly into the air, while the dog bellied down, ears still laid back, and eyed the trapper fearfully.

Releasing the man's wrist, Hardin said, "Now calm down, mister. I'll get him loose. You shouldn't be so rough with him—or so quick to kill him. Just back off and let me handle it."

The trapper sniffed derisively as he jammed the gun in its holster. "Go ahead, Marshal, but I hope you're prepared to get your arm chewed off. You're a stranger, too." As the man spoke he backed up several steps.

Turning toward the huge dog, Cougar stood about six feet away and spoke to the animal soothingly. "Now, big fella, I know those steel jaws are hurting you something awful. How about letting me set you free?"

Regarding his questioner with trusting eyes, the huge black dog raised up on its feet. Its ears came up and the fear left its eyes.

Hunkering down and inching closer, Hardin extended his right hand, palm upward, and said softly, "See, fella? There's nothing in my hand to hurt you. Okay?"

The dog whimpered, looked down at its trapped leg, then back at Cougar. Moving closer, Cougar slowly extended his open hand toward the dog's head.

"Better watch it, Marshal!" shouted the trapper. "He'll take your hand off!"

Over his shoulder Hardin said evenly, "I told you to let me handle it. He's not going to bite me."

The trapper scowled as he took several more steps backward.

Slowly Cougar placed his hand on the dog's head and patted it gently. "See, boy? I'm your friend. Nobody's going to hurt you as long as I'm here."

The dog whimpered again, and its tail began to wag. "That's it," Hardin said, his voice encouraging. "You understand, don't you?"

As the dog emitted yet another whimper, the animal-wise lawman calmly and methodically opened the jaws of the trap. Holding them open, he looked the dog square in the eye and said, "Okay, boy, pull your leg out."

The dog obeyed, but it did not turn and run off as Cougar had expected. Rather, it raised the injured paw for its rescuer to examine. Taking hold of the leg above the cut, Hardin looked it over. "You're all right, boy," he said softly. "Just lick the wound and the bleeding will stop. Before long it'll be as good as new."

As if it understood, the huge black animal gave a soft whine of appreciation, then licked its leg once. Glaring briefly at the trapper, the dog then limped away into the forest.

The marshal watched until it had disappeared from sight, then grinned at the trapper and said, "Years ago my stepmother taught me something that Solomon wrote in the Bible: 'A soft answer turneth away wrath, but grievous words stir up anger.' It might be good if you'd learn that lesson, mister."

The trapper did not answer.

Cougar quietly turned and walked through the trees back to his horse. Mounting up, he rode past the trapper and headed on down the mountain.

When dawn broke over the Bighorns, Gordo Silcox was already up, building a fire for cooking breakfast. The hunters and their captive had traveled southeast through the dense forest until late afternoon the day before, when it had become apparent that Jonathan could ride no farther. Hauling up beside a small brook, Silcox said they would make camp for the night. He had assigned Veronica to tend to his wounded son in spite of her injured leg, saying that Jonathan would have to be able to ride again by morning. They had to keep moving to stay ahead of Cougar, who no doubt was already on their trail.

Throwing off the blanket Silcox had taken from the Hardin home and that she had wrapped around her during her sleepless night, Veronica Simmons rose and glanced at the huge man building the fire, then limped painfully to Jonathan, who lay nearby under a blanket. Her right knee was swollen to nearly twice its normal size, and she had numerous bruises on her body.

Checking the packing that she had placed on the bullet hole in the back of Jonathan's left shoulder, Veronica found it soaked with blood. The bullet was buried deep, and it would have to come out soon or the young man would die.

Silcox looked over at his prisoner and asked, "How is he?"

"Not good," she replied, rising and putting her weight on the good leg. "He needs a doctor."

"Yeah, Pa," said Jonathan weakly, "you gotta go get me a doc. I can't ride no more."

The gang leader railed at his son, "Don't tell me you can't ride no more! We gotta keep movin'! You'll just have to tough it out till we can find the right spot to hole up in and ambush Cougar. When that's done, we'll get you to a doctor." Silcox called over to George Lang, who was bathing his face with cold water from the brook, asking gruffly, "Have *you* got any objections to my plan?"

Lang turned his blistered face toward Veronica, and the look he gave her was one of pure loathing. He then looked at Silcox and shook his head. "Nope. None at all."

A half hour later, while the two able-bodied men were hoisting Jonathan onto his horse, Veronica mounted her horse painfully and slowly, then gazed to the north. She knew Will Hardin would be heavy with grief, having found his family dead yesterday evening. But he would come to her rescue. She was sure of it.

After riding for just over an hour, with Jonathan doubled over in his saddle, they reached flat ground. There the trees thinned out, and the riders turned due south on a wagon-rutted trail. "Exactly where are we goin', Gordo?" asked Lang.

Silcox was about to answer when the sudden roar of a rifle shot rattled across the hills, coming from behind them to the north. The giant pulled rein and looked back over his shoulder.

"Probably a hunter," mused Lang, looking back as well.

"Maybe," Silcox ventured.

"I guarantee you it wasn't Cougar," spoke up the weary blonde. "If he were shooting at you, you'd all be on the ground dead by now."

Gordo Silcox set his narrow eyes on her, then bared his teeth and ordered, "Shut up! I'm the one who's makin' the guarantees—and I guarantee I'm gonna take care of your lover boy." Then he looked her up and down, adding with a smirk, "Soon as we're done runnin' and I got my boy all taken care of, you and me is gonna have a good time, my girl. You just think about that and let the anticipation build."

Veronica glared at him, refusing to let him see her fear. *I'd sooner be dead than let you put one repulsive finger on me*, she thought. *But I know that somehow Will is going to save me. He's just got to.*

As they moved forward, Lang asked again, "Exactly where is it we're goin'?"

"Well, I was thinkin' that we can take over one of the small ranches around here. In case Hardin's followin' us and tracks us there, we can set up an ambush and be ready for him. You've pretty much recovered—though your face *is* one unholy mess—so we'll have a much easier time of takin' him down. Once we've filled him full of lead, we'll haul Jonathan to the doc down in Buffalo."

He then looked at Veronica and shrugged, adding, " 'Course, maybe your boyfriend's too busy grievin' for his ma and pa to come lookin' for you. If so, we'll just stay in

some nice folks' house long enough for Jonathan to get
some rest, and then we'll move on. In that case, them nice
folks wouldn't have nothin' to worry about"—he gave her
a warning look—"so long as you don't say nothin' to 'em
that would force us to kill 'em." Silcox smiled wickedly.
"But a sweet thing like you, you wouldn't want blood on
your hands, now would you?"

They rode on another few minutes, then heard a rattling
sound behind them. Twisting in their saddles, they saw a
wagon topping a hill about a quarter of a mile behind
them, heading their way. It took only seconds for Veronica
to recognize the Appaloosa horses as those belonging to
Paul Welton, the father of her student Kathy. She knew
that the Weltons lived a short distance off to the southeast, and she thought of what Silcox had said earlier about
taking over a small ranch. Her heart turned to lead and
her face went chalky. Welton was going to ride right into a
trap.

"I'd say we got us a rancher comin', Gordo," Lang
remarked with a chuckle. "He must live somewhere close
by. Let's get the jump on him."

Silcox peered at Veronica. "Hey, girlie," he grunted. "I
could tell by the look on your face that you know this guy
that's comin'. Right?"

The wagon was close enough now that she could recognize the driver as Welton. There was no point in evading
the question. The rancher would be upon them in less
than a minute. "Yes, I know him," she replied with appre-
hension detectable in her voice. "His name is Paul Welton,
and he's the father of one of my pupils."

"Rancher, right?"

"Yes."

"Looks like our luck is changin', boys," Silcox snickered. Facing the fearful blonde, he told her, "I'm warnin'
you. You better go along with everything I say and put on
a good show, 'cause if you don't, this nice Mr. Welton will
die right here and right now. Got it?"

Veronica shifted slightly in the saddle, then winced

from the pain in her knee. "I understand," she said softly, knowing that pleading with him not to take over the Welton ranch would be useless.

"And you better hope for the Weltons' sake that your boyfriend don't show up before we're ready to move on. Otherwise things could get mighty nasty."

Paul Welton drew up alongside the riders, and a freshly killed deer was in the wagon bed. It was obvious that it had been he who had recently fired the rifle. Hauling his wagon to a stop, the young rancher cast a wary eye at the scurrilous-looking men, letting his gaze settle briefly on the bleeding Jonathan Silcox.

He then smiled at Veronica and said, "Good morning, Miss Simmons."

Veronica smiled weakly and responded, "Good morning, Mr. Welton."

Suddenly Welton's face pinched with concern. Peering more closely at her bruised face, he asked, "What happened to you?"

Replying for her, Gordo Silcox said, "It's kind of a long story, Mr. Welton. You see—"

"You know my name?" the rancher asked in surprise.

"Veronica just told us when she saw you drivin' up. Anyway, late yesterday afternoon, me and my friend and my son were at the Hardin place to pick up some knives we had ordered. Veronica had been visitin' the Hardins, and we offered to escort her back to her home. Just as it was growin' dark, a coyote ran across our path. I guess you know about the bounty on coyote pelts around these parts, right?"

"Yes," Welton allowed, clearly listening intently.

"Well, my friend here—George—was about to shoot that there coyote, but his horse shied just as George was pullin' the trigger. My son, Jonathan, was ridin' ahead of George, and when the horse shied, George's gun hand jerked up. The gun fired, and the bullet struck my boy in the shoulder. The sudden shot then scared Veronica's horse, and it jumped unexpectedly. She was thrown to the ground and wrenched her knee somethin' bad. Bruised her up some, too."

Welton was shaking his head in sympathy with Veronica as Silcox proceeded, "Well, we needed to get our injured to the doc in Sheridan as fast as possible, so we tried to find our way outta the mountains in the dark. Somehow we got off the path, and after a while we realized we was mixed up, so we camped for the night. When daylight came, Veronica looked around, tryin' to get her bearin's. When she finally realized where we were, and how far we was from Sheridan, she told us the best thing we could do was head for a nearby ranch where she knew the people . . . meanin' you. We was aimin' for your place when you came drivin' up."

The rancher gazed warily at the giant for a long moment. Then he looked at Veronica for confirmation, and when she nodded, he visibly relaxed, evidently accepting the story. "My place is only about a mile from here, right over that ridge," Welton said to Silcox. "Why doesn't your friend go for Doc Sibley while the rest of you come back with me?"

"Yeah, that's a good idea," Gordo Silcox allowed after a moment or two of thought. He had obviously concluded that since Veronica held the Weltons' lives in her hands, she would not say anything that would endanger them. Thanking the rancher for his kindness, Silcox led George Lang away from the wagon and, in a voice too low for Welton to hear, told his cohort, "No doubt the doc'll recognize you from descriptions of us. That bein' the case, force him at gunpoint to go with you—and warn him that if he says one word to the Weltons about who we are, they'll all die." Raising his voice, he added for the rancher's benefit, "While you're at it, get the doc to take a look at them burns." He turned to the rancher and explained, "George managed to scald himself yesterday. A real stupid accident." He laughed wryly, adding, "I guess you might say our luck ain't been none too good, huh?"

Paul Welton smiled sympathetically. "I guess not."

*   *   *

When the group reached the Welton ranch, Sarah Welton was told the same lies, and believing them just as her husband had, she welcomed the travelers into her home. She guided them to a large room that served as both parlor and kitchen, and after offering Jonathan Silcox the couch, she then helped Veronica to a large overstuffed chair and propped the young woman's foot on a stool. While her husband looked on, Sarah proceeded to put a fresh compress on Jonathan's wound.

Ten-year-old Kathy Welton sat on the arm of her teacher's chair, eyeing the ruffians fearfully, while her little brother, Bobby, who was five, hovered close to his mother. Paul Welton sat on a straight-backed chair near the outside door as Gordo Silcox paced back and forth, stopping periodically to peer out the windows.

Watching him, Veronica Simmons knew that Silcox feared that Will Hardin would show up before he had had time to set up an ambush. For that he would need George Lang, but it was imperative that Lang bring the doctor for Jonathan first.

When Silcox stopped pacing to look through a window for about the tenth time, Welton smiled and suggested, "Why don't you sit down and rest, Mr. Silcox? George and Doc Sibley won't be here for at least another hour."

Silcox shook his head, explaining, "I'm too concerned for my son. I wouldn't be able to sit still."

Veronica silently prayed. Hard though it was, she knew she could not expose the killers, for if she did, Silcox would certainly kill all the Weltons—including the children. She also feared for Dr. Ben Sibley, for if he had seen the buffalo hunters when they were in town, he would know they were the ones who had beaten up Red Wolf. *Oh, Will, please hurry,* she thought to herself. *Hurry!*

Not long after ten o'clock in the morning George Lang came riding into the yard with Ben Sibley following in his

one-horse carriage. Veronica studied Sibley's eyes when
he entered the house, certain she would be able to tell if
he knew whom he was dealing with. The look in them said
that he did. She started to speak, but he quickly shook his
head, and she held her tongue.

Sibley greeted the Weltons and was quickly led to Jonathan Silcox. After a brief examination, the physician told
Gordo Silcox that the bullet had to come out immediately.
Sibley gave the youth some laudanum and waited a few
minutes for the opiate to take effect. He then instructed
the men to lay Jonathan facedown on the trestle table in
the kitchen and prepared to dig the bullet out of his
shoulder.

The physician did his work under the watchful eye of
Gordo Silcox. When the surgery was completed and a
groggy Jonathan Silcox was placed back on the couch, Doc
Sibley told the anxious father, "Mr. Silcox, your son has
lost a lot of blood, and I'm afraid the bullet did extensive
damage in his shoulder. He also has a high fever, putting
him in serious danger."

The physician crossed the room to Veronica and asked
her how she had injured her knee and exactly where it
hurt. Pulling up a chair, he listened to her false explanation of how she was injured, and then he looked at it.
"That knee is swollen pretty badly, young lady. I'm afraid
I've got to cut the leg of your breeches to examine it.
Okay?"

"Whatever you have to do, Doctor," she responded.

He opened his medical bag and extracted a pair of
scissors. After cutting away some material, he gently ma-
nipulated Veronica's leg. When he had finished the examination, he said, "You have a severe sprain in this knee,
Veronica. You'll have to stay off the leg for at least two
weeks, and it must be kept elevated as much as possible
and soaked in cool water."

Smiling weakly, Veronica said, "I appreciate your help,
Dr. Sibley."

"I'd be happy to take you home in my buckboard," Paul Welton spoke up.

Gordo Silcox left his son's side. Throwing aside all pretense, he pulled his gun, cocked it, and bellowed sharply, "Stay where you are, Welton! Nobody's leavin' here!"

Chapter Eight

Taking his cue from his cohort, George Lang drew his gun and stepped beside Gordo Silcox, sweeping his hard-eyed gaze over the others in the room. Kathy and Bobby Welton both cried out, wrapping their arms fearfully around their mother, who was staring incredulously at the buffalo hunters. Paul Welton's face blanched as he asked, "What's this all about?"

"These men are outlaws," Dr. Ben Sibley answered grimly. "I had a bad feeling about them the minute I saw them, and I knew they were lying when I took the slug out of Jonathan's shoulder. That young man hadn't been shot with a revolver. The slug came from a rifle."

Veronica's heart was pounding and her breath was tight in her lungs as she looked at Silcox and implored, "Mr. Silcox, please don't hurt these people. Take me with you if you must, but don't stay here. You can make better time if you leave Jonathan here with Doc, and then you can be certain that he won't die."

Silcox's cheeks flushed. "You shut up, girl! Are you forgettin' he'd die anyway if the law got him? No, we're stayin' right here till your boyfriend shows up." He looked around, adding, "This setup'll do just fine for the ambush me and George are gonna set up for him."

Paul Welton stepped protectively beside his wife, then asked Veronica, "What's this all about?"

Her voice catching, the schoolteacher told the other captives about the gang's thirst for revenge against Will Hardin that had resulted in the gruesome murders of his entire family. There was shocked silence for a long moment, then Doc Sibley asked, "So what happens to us if you're able to succeed in ambushing Cougar?"

"I don't know," Silcox growled. "I haven't thought that far ahead." He suddenly smiled salaciously. "But I can tell you that blondie here is gonna come with me. I can use a good-lookin' young thing like her."

Veronica felt her blood go cold, and she had to look away as the revulsion she felt turned her stomach. Her mind began racing as she considered her impending fate, but she was pulled from her horrid thoughts by Silcox's shouting, "Hey, girl! Close them curtains so's your boyfriend can't see nothin'."

Facing the giant, she asked, "What?"

"I said close them curtains!" the buffalo hunter repeated. "When Cougar shows up, I don't want him seein' in so's he knows what we're up to. Hurry!"

Almost as if in a trance, Veronica Simmons limped around to all the windows and pulled the muslin curtains closed. When she had finished, she crossed the room and stood beside Ben Sibley, who put an arm around her shaking shoulders and tried to reassure her.

Silcox demanded of the rancher, "Is your rifle still out in the wagon with that dead deer?"

"Yes."

Glancing at George Lang, Silcox ordered, "Go get it."

Lang nodded and scurried out the door. Silcox then asked Welton, "Got any more guns in the house?"

Swallowing hard, Welton replied, "There's another rifle over there in the pantry."

George Lang returned, rifle in hand. "Okay," Silcox told him, a smile playing on his hard, ugly face, "let's plan how we're gonna take down Cougar."

*   *   *

Doggedly following the buffalo hunters' trail, Marshal Will Hardin had realized that it was leading to the Welton ranch. Just before a bend in the road, beyond which he knew the ranch house was visible, he had guided his horse into the woods. There he had dismounted and tied his horse, then hurried through the trees until he had neared the edge of the clearing that was Paul Welton's yard. He had studied the horses and vehicles arrayed in the yard, and aside from three unfamiliar horses, he identified Doc Sibley's carriage, the Welton's buckboard—and Veronica Simmons's dappled gray mare.

Suddenly a man had come out the front door, holstering his gun and moving toward the rancher's wagon. Hardin had immediately recognized the rail-thin body and the ratlike face of George Lang. Lang lifted a rifle off the front seat of the buckboard and stood looking at it with admiring eyes. Then Gordo Silcox shouted from the house, and Lang hurried back inside.

The young marshal scrutinized the situation. The killers had apparently been heading south with Veronica when Paul Welton, who had been deer hunting, rode up on them. From the amount of blood Cougar had found at the killers' campsite, Hardin had concluded that the bullet Obadiah had put in Jonathan Silcox had not killed him, but he was bleeding profusely and was no doubt in bad shape. Taking advantage of the rancher's proximity, the killers had holed up in the Welton house, and Doc Sibley was there to tend to Jonathan.

Cougar made a dash for the side of the house and crouched down under one of the open windows. Although the curtains had been drawn, he could clearly hear the voices from inside. After trying to decide what to do for several minutes and hearing Veronica plead with the killers to leave, Cougar suddenly heard her shout, "Get your filthy hands off me! I'd sooner die than be touched by you!"

"Is that so?" Silcox roared, his voice like the bellow of an angry bull. "Well, maybe I'll just give you your wish!" The buffalo hunter then cursed at Veronica and slapped her repeatedly, and her cries were like the lash of a whip in Will Hardin's mind. Fury welled up within him, and although a small voice within warned him not to race impetuously into the house but to wait until the killers came out before making his move, the fury he was feeling at Veronica's being manhandled drove him to take immediate action.

Throwing all caution aside, he drew his gun, rounded the house, and burst through the door. George Lang was just inside, holding his revolver on Ben Sibley and the Weltons, while Silcox was still slapping Veronica, her wrists held tightly in his free hand.

At the sight of Cougar the giant stayed his hand and shouted, and Lang whipped around, training his pistol on the intruder. But the agile lawman shot out his foot and kicked the gun out of Lang's grasp, and Ben Sibley immediately grabbed it and trained it on Lang. Hardin then swung his Colt. 45 on Silcox, but it was too late. The buffalo hunter had Veronica locked in his arm, the muzzle of his cocked revolver jammed into her ribs.

Will Hardin froze.

"Drop the gun, Cougar!" warned Silcox. "Drop it, or I'll kill her!"

Cougar knew if he dropped the gun, he and everyone else would be murdered. Gripping the Colt, he rasped angrily, "You're not going to kill her, Silcox, and I'm keeping my gun to make sure you don't."

"I tell you, I'll kill her!" spat the huge man.

"Not as long as I've got this gun! 'Cause you know I'll kill you if you shoot her!"

Silcox licked his lips and his eyes darted from Cougar to Lang. It was obvious that the standoff had him in a bind. Pulling his arm tighter around his hostage, he told his henchman, "Go help Jonathan up, George. We're gettin' outta here—and I'm takin' blondie with us to make sure her boyfriend don't try nothin' stupid."

Indicating Cougar, he continued, "And this guy's faster'n heat lightning, so don't try nothin' with him. Take Jonathan out to his horse and put him in the saddle. When you're ready to ride, holler."

Will Hardin's mind was racing. Silcox had the edge on him, and the man was desperate enough to shoot Veronica if he felt he was in a corner. Cougar was going to have to let them go.

Veronica looked at the lawman, and her expression told him that she knew that as long as the huge killer held her tightly in his grasp, pressing the muzzle of his gun into her, there was nothing Hardin could do. She shifted her head slightly, glancing at the Weltons, who stood in a tight knot, the children clinging to their parents. Then she looked back at Hardin. She was silently telling the lawman that it was best for everyone if he did what the killers demanded.

Ben Sibley stood near the couch where Lang was struggling to hoist a torpid Jonathan Silcox to his feet. Silcox shouted, "Help him, Doc!"

Sibley frowned and retorted, "He shouldn't be moved. You'll kill him if you do!"

"He's tough," countered Silcox. "He'll make it. You just do as I tell you." Glaring at Will Hardin, he said, "And you better do as I tell you, too! If you follow us, if I see hide or hair of you, I'll kill her."

Kathy Welton started crying, and she buried her face in her mother's skirt. Glaring at the child, Silcox commanded, "Shut the brat up! She's gettin' on my nerves." Sarah Welton knelt and hugged her daughter, speaking soothingly to her.

Cougar's face darkened with anger and frustration, but he checked his impulse to leap across the space that separated them and bash the giant's face with his fist. He knew that any kind of jolt could drop the hammer on Silcox's gun, and Veronica would be shot.

Silcox regarded the lawman with cold eyes, then told him, "As soon as we get outta this part of the country to where we feel safe, we'll release her."

"And why should I believe you?"

Silcox smiled slowly. "You don't have much choice, do you, Hardin? Although I can shoot her right now if you prefer."

"No!" Cougar shouted.

Shrugging, the giant said easily, "Okay. You stay away, and I'll let her live."

Will Hardin had no intention of giving in to the murderer's demands, but all he said was, "If you harm her, this world isn't big enough to hide you."

George Lang's voice suddenly rang out. "We're ready to ride, Gordo!"

Still holding the cocked revolver against Veronica's body, Silcox half-carried and half-dragged the young woman toward the door as Cougar and the Weltons watched helplessly. Hardin followed at a safe distance, indicating he would not try anything, and watched as Silcox adeptly placed Veronica in his own saddle, then mounted up behind her. The entire time he kept the gun trained on her so that if Cougar were to shoot him, reflex action would fire the giant's gun.

Ben Sibley stepped onto the porch and stood beside Will Hardin. George Lang grabbed the reins of Jonathan Silcox's horse to lead it, and with the group ready to ride, Gordo Silcox stared menacingly at Hardin and growled, "I'm tellin' you one more time. Don't follow . . . or she dies."

Veronica looked at Cougar, terror written on her lovely face. A hot lump welled up in Hardin's throat, and a sinking sensation washed over him like icy water. He desperately wanted to tell her that he was in love with her, but these circumstances were not right for it. Scolding himself for charging into the house, Hardin thought that if he had just heeded the warning voice in his head, Veronica might now be free. Instead, his impetuousness had placed him in a helpless position and further endangered Veronica's life.

When Gordo Silcox nudged his horse's flanks and began leading his men south, a quiver of panic shot through Cougar's stomach. Then he remembered something that Red Wolf had said to him during many of their hunting excursions: *"Be patient, my grandson. The mark of a good hunter is patience."* Cougar steeled himself against the panic and thought, *Patience, Will! You'll get her back safe and sound. Just be patient, and when you follow, the right moment to free her will come.*

The buffalo hunters were already heading down the road when Cougar could not contain his feelings for Veronica any longer. She had to know. Cupping his hands around his mouth, he called loudly, "Ronnie! I love you!"

Veronica twisted against Gordo Silcox's strong hold on her and looked back at the man she loved, then burst into tears.

Soon the scurrilous men and their hostage were out of sight. Cougar wheeled around, and there was fire in his steel-gray eyes as he told Doc Sibley and the Weltons, who were huddled on the porch, "I'm going to follow them without their knowing it till it's too late. They'll pay for their crimes, and Ronnie will be rescued."

"I'll go with you," offered Paul Welton.

"Thanks, but I'll say to you what I said to Ronnie's father: One man can stay out of sight a whole lot easier than two."

"I understand," Welton murmured, nodding.

"They're not going to get far with that young man as bad off as he is, Will," Doc Sibley remarked. "He's not going to make it."

"That means that I need to get on their tails right away, 'cause they'll travel faster once he dies."

Kathy Welton suddenly rushed over to Will Hardin and asked tearfully, "You *will* bring Miss Simmons back, won't you, Mr. Cougar? She's the best teacher in all the world."

"I sure will, Kathy," the young marshal replied, smiling reassuringly at her. "That's a promise." With that, he started back into the woods for his horse.

He had almost reached his mount when he saw ahead of him the huge black dog he had rescued from certain death in the mountains. The animal was ambling toward him, wagging its long, fluffy tail.

Surprised to see the dog, Cougar knelt down and stroked its ponderous head. "Hey, big fella. What are you doing here? I guess you belong to the Weltons, huh? I bet Kathy and Bobby will be glad to have you home."

After petting the dog for a few moments, he continued toward his horse, then mounted up. Leading the horse through the woods to where the timber met the road, the lawman looked cautiously before leaving his cover, making certain his prey could not see him. Once he had established that he could safely follow, Hardin nudged his mount onto the road.

Sensing he was not alone, Cougar looked back and was surprised to see that the dog was following him. "Go on home, fella," he instructed. The animal sat down, watching as Cougar trotted away. It was still sitting there watching him, a black dot against the dusty road, when Hardin looked over his shoulder one last time before dropping into a shallow valley.

While his father led them in a gallop for several miles, Jonathan Silcox gripped the saddlehorn, barely staying on his horse. Suddenly he shouted, "Pa! Pa! I gotta stop! I can't go no farther!"

Gordo Silcox slowed his horse to a brisk walk, looking back. Jonathan was as pale as a ghost, and his face was dripping with sweat. Reining in, Silcox signaled for George Lang to halt and let Jonathan's horse stop beside him. Gaunt and haggard, his eyes more vapid than ever, Jonathan sleeved sweat from his face and gasped, "I'm sick,

Pa. My head's spinnin' somethin' terrible. I can't ride no more."

"Look, son," the buffalo hunter argued, "I know you're real bad, but we gotta keep movin'. We just gotta keep movin'! I got a feelin' that lawman's gonna pull somethin' on us." Looking nervously back down the road, the massive killer sighed. "Okay. We'll rest for a few minutes. But then we'll head out again. I'm aimin' for Buffalo. There's bound to be a doctor there. If we can keep goin', we'll get there sometime tomorrow."

"If we keep going, he won't be alive tomorrow," Veronica Simmons declared tartly.

"Shut up!" growled Gordo. "I didn't ask for your opinion!" Looking back at his son, he said, "Just a few minutes, Jonathan. That's all we can afford."

Ten minutes later, they were on the move again.

Casting a hopeful look at their back trail, Veronica heard Cougar's last words echoing over and over in her mind. She wondered in what light Will Hardin had meant his words of love. They had been friends for a long time, but he had never before said that he loved her. Did he mean it the way it sounded? Was that possible after all these years? After all the times she had dreamed he—

"Hopin' your boyfriend's gonna follow us, huh?" Silcox snickered, interrupting her thoughts. "Well, you better pray he don't. If he does, you'll die."

Swallowing hard, the young woman faced forward, blinking back her tears. *No!* she thought angrily, refusing to give in to her hopelessness. *Somehow I will survive this, and Will and I will be reunited. Fate would not be that cruel to have him finally realize his love for me only to have me die.*

It was sundown, and there had been no sign of Cougar all day. Gordo Silcox led his group into the bottom of a gully, where they made camp for the night and ate supper. In spite of her pain, Veronica Simmons was forced to do the cooking and the cleaning up afterward. Silcox also made her tend his son's wound.

Silcox and Lang traded off keeping watch through the night. The next morning, Jonathan was so weak he could not eat, but he was nonetheless hoisted onto his horse. Shortly after nine o'clock they passed through Dry Creek, a small settlement made up of a few shanties and tents, and two of the makeshift canvas structures housed the general store and the saloon.

Although George Lang wanted to stop and get a couple of drinks, Silcox refused the request. "If I ain't gonna stop so's my son can rest, I sure ain't gonna stop so you can toss back a couple," he admonished his cohort.

An hour out of Dry Creek, Lang heard a groan behind him. Twisting around in the saddle, he saw Jonathan fall to the ground. "Gordo! Jonathan's fallen! I think he's passed out!"

Lang quickly dismounted and knelt beside the young man. The fall had torn open the wound, and blood was oozing from it in a steady flow.

Silcox swore loudly. He glanced around, trying to decide what to do, and then suddenly pointed through the trees. "George, look! Over there in the woods up ahead! 'Pears like there's an old barn settin' all by itself, and from the looks of its dilapidated condition, I'd say it ain't bein' used." He looked back at his son, then sighed. "I guess we better hole up in there, 'cause we sure ain't gonna make it to Buffalo today. We'll take Jonathan and the girl to the barn, and then you ride back to Dry Creek and get food and whiskey." Then his eyes hardened, and he commanded, "But get back here as fast as you can. I don't want you doin' no hangin' around so's people'll remember you. Understand?"

"Yeah, Gordo. I understand."

The giant then looked down at his fallen son, and his expression turned to one of sadness. It was clear that he knew Jonathan Silcox was going to die—it was just a question of when.

Chapter Nine

Cougar Will Hardin doggedly trailed the Silcox gang and their captive as they wound their way through the rugged foothill country, heading south. Knowing that Jonathan Silcox was close to death, Hardin was careful not to ride too fast and get too close. If he could see them, they could also see him—and if that happened, Silcox might just keep his word and put a bullet in Veronica Simmons. Cougar had to bide his time and find a way to take them totally unaware.

There was a yearning in Cougar's heart for the beautiful young woman that he had never known before. Everything seemed to change within him once he realized that what he felt for her was love and not just friendship. Lashing himself, he thought, *Will Hardin, you have been without a doubt the blindest of the blind! And now that you've seen the light, now that you want to hold Ronnie in your arms and kiss her sweet lips, now that you yearn to whisper tender words of love into her ears, she is out of reach.*

Will Hardin shook his head, deciding that such regrets did neither him nor Veronica any good. He had to concentrate on freeing her . . . and then he would tell her a thousand times over how much he loved her.

Presently Dry Creek came into view ahead of him. He

held his horse at a steady trot until he was within two hundred yards of the settlement, then slowed to a walk, approaching the tents and shacks with caution. If Gordo Silcox and George Lang were stopped in Dry Creek, he did not want them to see him. His eyes darted back and forth as he rode along, and when he saw no sign of the killers or their horses, he decided to see if he could find out how long it had been since they had passed through.

Cougar spotted two elderly men sitting on wooden crates, whittling sticks and talking. He veered his horse over to their side of the dusty road, pulling rein a few feet from them. When his tall shadow fell on the pair, they looked up and broke off their conversation.

"Good morning, gentlemen," the young lawman said amiably.

Their eyes rested briefly on the star on his chest, and then they said in unison, "Mornin', Marshal."

The elder of the two asked, "Where're you marshal at, son?"

"Sheridan, sir," replied Hardin.

"Sheridan?" the old fellow repeated, arching his shaggy white eyebrows in surprise. "I thought Zack Traynor was marshal there."

Hardin's face stiffened. "He was until yesterday. He was murdered. Cut down in cold blood by buffalo hunters. My name's Will Hardin, and I was his deputy. The town made me marshal, and now I'm trailing the killers." Cougar then described the Silcox men, George Lang, and their captive, Veronica Simmons, asking if either of the oldsters had seen them.

The men eyed each other, shrugged, then shook their heads.

"How long have you been sitting here?" queried the young lawman.

The white-haired men looked at each other again, then the elder one said, "I'd say about an hour."

Nodding, Hardin mused, "Then they probably came

through before then." He looked around, then asked, "Know anyone who might be able to tell me more?"

"Well, you might try down at the tradin' post or the saloon, son," replied the younger of the pair. "Maybe them killers stopped and did some business in one of those places. They're both open at six in the mornin'."

"Much obliged," said the marshal, nudging his horse on down the road.

Farther along were two large tents that stood adjacent to one another. Crude signs in front of each designated one as the trading post and the other as the saloon. Several saddled horses and wagons stood around the two structures, and a group of men, women, and children were collected in front of the trading post. In front of the saloon a few laughing, animated men were gathered.

Hardin decided to try the saloon first, thinking that perhaps Silcox and Lang stopped long enough to have a few drinks. Dismounting, the marshal tied his horse and stepped around the group who milled in front of the tent and headed for the opening, a pinned-back flap.

The stench of sweaty, unbathed bodies, cigar smoke, and whiskey fumes assaulted Cougar's nostrils the instant he stepped inside the tent. Having come from the brilliant sunlight, he needed a few seconds to allow his eyes to adjust to the dimness, although small shafts of sunlight pierced the canvas where the tent had been punctured or torn, providing a bit more light.

At the end of the tent was the bar—a makeshift though solid-looking affair constructed of four posts, a wooden framework, and three very long, thick, rough-hewn planks nailed on top. Several men sat on wooden benches and barrels scattered about the tent; while some stood around in small groups, chatting. All held bottles or shot glasses. Cougar counted seven men at the bar, one of whom—a man who appeared to be a drifter—was loudly dominating the conversation.

When his eyes were fully adjusted to the gloom of the tent, Will Hardin angled toward the bar. A fat, bald-headed bartender stood behind it, eyeing his loudmouthed patron with naked contempt. Looking away from the patron, the bartender focused on the tall man with the badge on his chest who was walking slowly toward him, regarding the lawman with an expression of curiosity.

Cougar drew up behind the loudmouth, looked at the bartender, and said above the noise, "Howdy. I need to ask you a question."

"Sure, Marshal," the fat man said with a smile.

Suddenly the loudmouth pivoted, leaning his back against the bar. "Marshal?" he bellowed, echoing the bartender's last word and looking directly at the shiny star that Hardin wore. He then looked Cougar up and down, disdain evident on his grizzled face. Gazing levelly into Hardin's gray eyes, the man snickered, "Marshal of what? That star don't say 'U.S. Marshal,' so you must be marshal of some podunk cowtown hereabouts."

Cougar's square jaw hardened, and his voice was cold as he retorted, "I wasn't addressing you, mister. I was speaking to the bartender."

Glaring at the lawman, the man countered loudly, "My name ain't 'mister.' It's Luke Bascomb. And I'll say whatever I want, whenever I want. And no tin star's gonna tell me otherwise!"

Conversations died quickly in the tent, and suddenly every eye was aimed toward the bar. The tall, heavyset man beside the loudmouthed drifter nudged him in the ribs and remarked in a snide voice, "Hey, Luke, maybe you shouldn't get this tough hombre riled! Just look at that great big knife he's wearin', and lookee at the iron on his hip! Ooh! I'm real scared!"

Then the man on the other side of Bascomb pointed out, "Heck, he's such a skinny dude, I kinda wonder if he can even lift that heavy gun outta the holster!"

The loudmouth sneered and quipped, "Naw, Byrd. I'd say he's sportin' fancy gear hopin' nobody'd challenge him. More'n likely he's got a wide yellow streak." He looked at his other friend, asking, "What do you think, Mac?"

Mac Olden lifted his full shot glass, spilling some of its contents. Pointing the glass at Hardin, he announced, "I'd say you're right, Luke. Here's to all yellow-bellied lawmen who are nothin' but show!" Keeping his eyes fixed on Cougar, he tossed his drink down in one gulp.

Will Hardin was eager to get back on the trail. Fighting his rising anger, he ignored the snide remarks and said to the bartender, "My name is Will Hardin. I'm looking for three men and a woman who passed through here earlier this morning. The woman's young and blond, and the men—well, one of them's wounded real bad, one of them's tall and thin, and the man in charge is huge. He's somewhere in his forties, he's bearded, wears a buffalo-hide vest, and stinks to high heaven. Have you seen any of them?"

The bartender was about to respond when Olden looked sharply at Cougar and asked angrily, "You lawmen all take great pleasure chasin' somebody down, don't you? You think that badge gives you the right to make people miserable?"

Battling to control his temper, Hardin ran his cold gray gaze over the three hard-bitten faces and rasped, "I assume you mangy coyotes have had some kind of run-in with a lawman or two."

The leader of the trio stiffened. "Better be careful who you're callin' mangy coyotes!" he hissed. "Why don't you get on out of here and head back to your hick town before you regret you ever stopped in Dry Creek?"

Will Hardin's nerves were stretching tight.

"Yeah," Mac Olden yelled, "get on out of here, 'cause the sight of your ugly, scarred face is makin' me sick!"

Will Hardin's open hand suddenly slammed hard against the man's chest. "You're pressing your luck," he breathed hotly. "I came in here for information, and you fools aren't going to prevent me from getting it. You three found your way in here; now I suggest you find your way out—quick!"

George Lang rode into Dry Creek, figuring he'd have time to get a couple of drinks at the saloon before buying the whiskey and food Gordo Silcox had sent him to pick up. Dismounting in front of the saloon tent, he ground-tied his horse alongside the other horses, whistling tune-lessly as he strode toward the tent. As he drew closer he wondered what was going on in the saloon that was hold-ing the interest of the men clustered around the flap, peering in.

He stepped up behind them and was about to ask them to move aside and let him enter when he heard a small boy shout, "Mama! Look at that big dog! Wow! That's the biggest dog I ever saw in my whole life!"

Lang turned and looked in the direction of the voice. The child was pointing to a huge black dog that was walking slowly down Dry Creek's main thoroughfare. The buffalo hunter idly studied the dog for a few seconds, then turned back to the tent. Tapping one man on the back who was blocking the way, he said, "Would you mind movin'? I'd like to get in there."

The man looked over his shoulder and suggested, "You might think twice about goin' in right now, mister. Looks like there's gonna be a fight. Might be some bullets'll fly."

Peering over the man's shoulder, George Lang sud-denly felt the blood drain from his face. Toward the back of the tent, squaring off with three drifters, was Cougar Will Hardin. The tall, rangy lawman was too busy with his adversaries to take notice of any spectators. Scrubbing a hand across his mouth, Lang noticed several tears in the sides of the tent and immediately backed away from the front and hurried around to the right side. There he positioned himself at one of the slits and anxiously watched the confrontation.

Clearly confident that the odds were well stacked in his favor, Luke Bascomb, the leader of the trio, snarled at Will Hardin, "Tell you what, Scarface, why don't you just throw us out?"

Cougar's cold gray stare did not waver. "I can do it if you insist," he said evenly.

Byrd and Olden stood poised and ready when Bascomb retorted dryly, "I insist."

The bartender and the other patrons quickly cleared well out of the way, giving the opponents room.

Inwardly cursing the drifters for interrupting his search for the buffalo hunters, Cougar nonetheless had been pushed too hard, and he could not back away from the challenge. Lunging with the swiftness of his namesake, he chopped Mac Olden in the Adam's apple with the blade of his left hand, then punched Kent Byrd savagely in the stomach, felling both of them. At the sight of his two friends going down, their loudmouthed leader swore and reached for his gun, but the lawman grabbed a nearly full whiskey bottle from the bar and smashed it against Bascomb's forehead. The drifter collapsed to the floor, unconscious.

Mac Olden struggled to his feet, gagging and choking, with murder in his eyes. He leapt at Hardin, but the lawman sidestepped him and chopped him on the ear. The man staggered slightly, then came at his opponent again, fists balled and ready for battle.

Ducking, Cougar let him swing both fists, then caught him with an uppercut that snapped his head back. Olden swayed momentarily, then came again, fists swinging. Cougar lithely dodged more blows and peppered him on the nose, driving him backward. When the man threw his hands up to protect himself, Hardin drove a violent blow to his belly, and breath gushed from the big man as he slid to his knees.

While his friend was down, Kent Byrd finally regained his feet and jumped on Cougar's back, locking his neck in the crook of his arm, a move that took the lawman by surprise. Rallying, Cougar flipped his burden over his head, slamming him hard on the ground. Byrd lay there, the wind knocked out of him, gasping for breath.

Meanwhile Olden lumbered to his feet, swearing vociferously. Sucking hard for air, he challenged, "Seems I heard you say you could throw us out! Well, there ain't one of us out of here yet, lawman!"

"There will be," Hardin promised, moving in close to his foe.

Cougar and Olden began trading blows. With his attention on his immediate adversary, the young marshal did not notice that Kent Byrd was once again standing and was slowly reaching for his gun. Then the two men trading punches abruptly shifted positions, and Will Hardin got a clear look at the gun in Byrd's hand. The drifter was hesitating, and it was apparent by the look on his scruffy face that he was reluctant to fire for fear he might hit his friend.

Ducking away from Olden, Cougar's right hand dropped to his waist. Suddenly there was a flash of silver as he threw his knife with deadly accuracy, burying its blade in Byrd's throat. The man stiffened and let the pistol drop. Then both hands went to the knife handle while his startled eyes stared in disbelief. He staggered a few steps, reeled, and collapsed, gagging and coughing for several seconds before he died. Some of the men who looked on put their hands to their throats instinctively and shuddered.

"You murdered my pal!" Mac Olden screamed. "You ain't livin' through this, lawman!" As he spoke he clawed for his gun, but he looked down with surprise to discover it had tumbled out of the holster when he had fallen. Roaring like a wild beast, he charged at Cougar, his head down so as to catch Cougar in the midsection. The lawman, who stood with his back to the bar, stepped aside a split second before the big man reached him, and Olden slammed head-on into the solid bar.

Stunned, the drifter wobbled two steps back, blinking and trying to clear his vision. A wide gash split his forehead from where it had struck the sharp edge of the bar. Eyes wild with fury, he reached for Hardin, but the marshal sank his strong fingers into the man's hair. The onlookers winced as Hardin repeatedly slammed his foe's head into the bar. Suddenly the big man's body went limp, and when Cougar released him, Mac Olden went down in a heap like a rag doll.

Breathing hard, the lawman turned to the bartender. After catching his breath, he remarked, "I don't think you ever got a chance to answer me. Did you see any of the people I described?"

"No, sir," the bartender answered, staring at the sinewy young lawman, clearly astonished by his physical prowess.

Cougar strode over to Kent Byrd's body and pulled his knife from the dead man's throat. Wiping the blade clean on Byrd's shirt, the lawman inserted it back into its sheath, then walked back to the bartender, who was kneeling over Mac Olden.

"He's dead, Marshal," the fat man advised him. "You crushed his skull."

"Yeah," Cougar muttered, "I know."

"You sure did a job on that bunch, Marshal!" spoke up one of the patrons.

Casting a glance toward the man, Hardin pointed out, "My job's not finished yet. I promised I would throw them out of here."

The crowd at the tent opening cleared a path for Will Hardin as he dragged the two bodies out of the tent. Returning inside, he stood over Luke Bascomb, the drifter who had started the fight and who had finally come to.

Outside, still peering through the slit in the side of the tent, George Lang stood with his mouth agape, obviously awestruck by Will Hardin's fighting ability. When the marshal once again went into the tent, the buffalo hunter hurried to his horse, swung into the saddle, and rode fast out of Dry Creek back toward the deserted barn.

Inside the tent, Luke Bascomb glared at the lawman with obvious hate in his murky eyes, but he said nothing. Cougar reached down and pulled him to his feet, then held him nose to nose for a long moment, glaring at him. He then let go, but Bascomb's legs were not quite ready to hold him, and the drifter grabbed the edge of the bar and leaned against it. Cougar gave him a hard look, then wheeled and stepped out into the sunlight.

He stopped a few other people and asked them if they

had seen the buffalo hunters and Veronica Simmons. After receiving nothing but negative replies, the lawman headed for his horse.

As Will Hardin made his way to his mount, he was surprised to see the huge black dog whose life he had saved lying next to the horse. As soon as the dog spotted Hardin, it jumped up, wagging its tail. Shaking his head, the marshal grinned, and when he reached the dog, he knelt down to pet it. Taking the dog's big, broad head into his hands, he rubbed the shaggy ears with his thumbs and said, "Now, listen, big fella. I had a dog once, but he got killed. I really don't want another one. You came from somewhere, so go on home."

The dog whined as Hardin stepped into the stirrup and eased into the saddle. Looking down at the huge animal, he said affectionately, "Hey, fella, don't even try to persuade me. I've got enough on my mind without worrying about taking care of a big ugly mutt."

Looking up at Cougar with sad brown eyes, the black beast whined again. "Don't give me that look," Cougar quipped, laughing. "It isn't going to work. I'm telling you, I don't want another dog—especially one that's so all-fired ugly. Now, you go on about your business so I can take care of mine."

Touching his spurs to his horse's flanks, Hardin headed south. Just before he left Dry Creek, the lawman looked back. The dog was sitting in the middle of the street, watching him go.

The young lawman thought back to the puppy Obadiah had given him when he was six years old. Ruff had been his best friend for most of his childhood years, and Hardin once again felt the pain and horror he had experienced when he had dashed from the cabin to find his good friend clawed to death by the big cat—and once again he felt the rage. Suddenly he was aware of the rage he was feeling now toward the buffalo hunters for murdering his family and abducting Veronica. Only this time, the rage was even hotter and much more intense.

* * *

Luke Bascomb leaned on the bar in the tent saloon for several minutes while he regained his strength. When he was sure he could walk without collapsing, he picked up his fallen hat, dropped it on his head, and left the tent. Pushing his way through the crowd that was gathered around his two dead friends, he stood over them. He knelt beside them and went through their pockets, pulling out several bills and coins. Blood dripped from the gash on his head into his eyes, and he pulled a dirty bandanna from his hip pocket and dabbed at his bleeding head. Looking up from his friends, he watched the lawman ride away.

With murder in his eyes Bascomb muttered through clenched teeth, "I'm gonna kill you, Scarface! You can bet on it!"

The bartender was standing at the open flap of his tent as Luke Bascomb approached. "I heard that threat," the fat man announced, a scowl on his moon-shaped face, "and if I were you, I'd think twice about taking that man on."

Regarding the bartender coldly, Bascomb growled, "Well, you ain't me! And if I wanted your advice, I'd have asked for it." When the bartender did not move, Bascomb frowned and said, "What I *do* want is another drink, and I want to talk to you."

The bartender shrugged and walked to the rear of the tent and stood behind the bar. Grabbing a bottle, he uncorked it and filled a shot glass. As he jammed the cork back in the neck of the bottle, he looked at his bleeding customer and asked, "If three of you couldn't handle him, how do you think you're goin' to do it all by your lonesome?"

Bascomb gave him a cold look, took a healthy swig from the glass, and retorted, "I have my ways."

A wide grin spread across the bartender's face. "I've been tendin' bar for nigh onto twenty-seven years. I've seen more fights than you can shake a stick at . . . and in all my days, I've never seen one man who could fight like that fella. I'm tellin' you, you'd best forget goin' after him."

Wicked, malevolent eyes bored into the bartender. Tossing the last of the whiskey down his throat, Bascomb banged the glass on the rough-hewn bar, then said, "Save your advice. You're only wastin' your breath. Now, what I want from you is to see to it that my friends are given a decent burial."

"That costs money," the barkeep said drily.

The drifter riffled the paper money he had taken from his dead cohorts, peeled off several bills, then slapped them on the bar. "There's thirty bucks. That oughtta buy two holes in the ground and a couple of pine boxes."

"Just about," the fat man agreed. "But what about my fee for seein' that it gets done?"

Bascomb swore under his breath as he extracted another bill. "Here's five bucks. That enough?"

Scooping up the money, the bartender promised, "I'll see that it's done. But you also owe me two bits for the drink."

Luke Bascomb's face turned purple. Jamming his hand into his pocket, he produced a quarter and smacked it on the bar.

The bald-headed bartender grinned and picked up the coin.

As Luke Bascomb walked toward the tent opening, the barkeep shouted after him, "Tell me somethin', mister. Who's gonna pay for *your* decent burial after Will Hardin kills *you*?"

Bascomb paused, looked over his shoulder, and snapped, "I'm gonna bring Hardin's rotten corpse in here and make you eat your words, barkeep!" Then he spat on the earthen floor and stormed outside, hurrying across the street.

The bartender grinned, took a clean shot glass from the counter, and poured himself a drink. Corking the bottle, he lifted the glass toward Luke Bascomb's retreating back and said, "Here's to your pipe dreams."

Chapter Ten

Will Hardin was about a half mile out of Dry Creek when he picked up the tracks of the buffalo hunters. The going was slow, for several wagons and other horses had traveled the road, and their tracks frequently obscured the distinct prints of the three horses. It was not until well over an hour after he had left the settlement that he came to the spot where the killers had left the road and headed into the woods.

Following the trail, Cougar rode into the deep shade, picking his way slowly through the forest. Suddenly he heard from behind him the angry whir of a bullet, and at virtually the same instant a gun roared. Then a vicious snarl cut the air, followed by a man's scream.

Hardin was out of his saddle in a flash, gun in hand. The snarling and screaming continued as the lawman raced back through the trees in the direction of the sounds. Abruptly he came upon Luke Bascomb, who was pinned to the ground by the huge black dog as the infuriated animal snapped and slashed at Bascomb's face with its teeth. The drifter's gun lay on the ground with thin tendrils of smoke coming from the muzzle. Hardin realized that he had heard the growl and the shot simultaneously, and he was sure that the dog had taken Bascomb by surprise and spoiled his aim, saving Will Hardin's life.

Bascomb's shrieks pierced the air as he twisted to and fro, trying to fight off the razor-sharp fangs that were ripping his face. Then the furious dog bit the would-be assassin's nose, puncturing it and shredding the flesh. Bascomb managed to ram an elbow into the dog's face, but he quickly found the powerful jaws savagely biting it. Grabbing the man's arm, the dog shook it vigorously.

Bascomb's terrified eyes met Hardin's cold ones. "Help me!" the man wailed. "Please! I beg of you! Help me!"

At Cougar's command, the dog stopped its attack. But its fangs bared and a deep growl rumbling in its throat, it continued to stand over the drifter, dripping saliva onto his face and pinning him to the ground.

Bascomb shook with terror. His face was a bloody mess as he begged, "Hardin, get him off me! Please!"

Cougar looked down impassively and asked, "Why should I? You tried to shoot me in the back. If my dog hadn't jumped you, you'd have killed me. Right?"

The horrified man was staring up at the deadly bared fangs poised just above his throat. "I . . . I—"

"Answer me!" demanded Hardin. "My dog kept you from killing me, didn't he?"

"Yes," Luke Bascomb whimpered.

Glaring at the drifter, Cougar rasped, "Give me one good reason why I should call him off."

Bascomb seemed numb with horror.

"Well, come on," taunted Hardin. "I'm waiting for a good reason. Seems to me I should tell him to rip you to shreds."

"No! No! You can't! You're a lawman!"

"I'd be a *dead* lawman right now if you'd had your way. But regardless, since lawmen are supposed to believe in justice, it seems to me that justice would be served if the man who tried to take my life loses his own." Shrugging, he added, "However, I'm a sporting man, so I'll tell you what. I'll ride off and leave you to my dog. If you can figure a way to get away from him, you'll live. Otherwise—"

"No!" Bascomb shrieked. "Don't leave!"

The outburst enraged the dog, and it snarled and snapped its jaws, spraying the drifter's bloody face with saliva. Bascomb's entire body shook like a leaf in an autumn wind. White with terror, he stared up at Cougar and whispered, "Please, Marshal. I . . . I'm sorry! Please don't leave me with your dog! I beg of you! Have mercy on me!"

Anxious to continue on the buffalo hunters' trail, Hardin responded coolly, "Who knows? My dog may be so mad at you that he won't listen to me. But let me see what I can do."

Backing away a few steps, the lawman slapped his thigh and said, "Okay, boy, come here."

The huge black animal looked at Hardin, looked back at the terrified man, then trotted to Hardin. It clearly thought of the lawman as its master.

Bascomb began to weep with relief. Sitting up, he pulled his bandanna from his hip pocket and dabbed at his lacerated face.

Stroking the dog's head, Cougar said to Bascomb, "You'd better mount up and ride for the nearest doctor. That would be at Fort Kearney a few miles due east of here. You know where it is?"

"Yeah," the drifter replied, his voice barely above a whisper.

"I should arrest you for attempted murder, but luckily for you I've got something more important to do."

As Luke Bascomb groped his way to his feet and stumbled in the brush toward his horse, Hardin warned him, "I'd better never see you again. Next time, I *will* let my dog kill you!" Then, remembering that Bascomb had called him Scarface, the marshal called, "Looks as if *you* will be a scarface now!"

Bascomb climbed slowly into his saddle and rode east without looking back. When he was out of sight, Cougar looked down and found that the dog was standing beside him. Kneeling, he hugged the animal's huge neck and got affectionately licked on the face. "Well, big fella," Cougar said softly, "looks as if you've evened things up. I saved your hide; now you've saved mine. Did you hear what I told that guy? I told him you were my dog. Do you want to be my dog?"

The huge black animal whined and looked fondly at Cougar, as if it understood. Patting the animal's ponderous head, Cougar chuckled. "You're a smart one, I'll give you that. You know what I'm saying, don't you?"

Ruffling the thick scruff on the dog's neck, he observed, "Don't know why anybody would want you. You're uglier than homemade sin. But from now on we're partners, old boy. Now, let's see . . . you've got to have a name." Thinking for a moment, he said, "Without your help, I'd be dead now. I guess that makes you my partner . . . my . . . my deputy. That's it! I hereby commission you as my deputy. And that will be your name."

Standing, the young marshal ordered, "Come on, Deputy! Let's go find Ronnie!"

Veronica Simmons sat on the barn floor beside the dying Jonathan Silcox, slowly pouring water from a canteen into his mouth. At first forced to tend the repulsive young man, Veronica soon realized that as long as he was alive, Jonathan's condition worked to keep Silcox at bay. For the buffalo hunter knew that if he touched her, she would no longer tend his son with such concern—so as long as the young man was still breathing, Gordo Silcox would not force himself on Veronica.

The giant sat a few feet away on the floor with his back against a post, biting off a chaw of tobacco. Staring at him with undisguised loathing, the schoolteacher told him, "Your son is bleeding to death. The stitches have ripped loose completely, and I can't get the bleeding stopped. If you want him to live, you've got to get him to a doctor. Take him back to Sheridan."

The buffalo hunter growled, "You'd better get it stopped 'cause there ain't no other alternative. I ain't gonna end up in jail takin' him to no doc."

"Well, then, there's an Army doctor at Fort Kearney," suggested the young woman. "Why not take him there? It's only a few miles away."

Shaking his head vigorously, Silcox shouted, "No! The Army's as bad as lawmen! You don't seem to get it, do you, sister? I got an aversion to jails, so I ain't puttin' myself in no position to end up behind bars."

Veronica's eyes pierced him as she asked coolly, "Even if it makes the difference between whether your son lives or dies?"

Silcox's ugly face turned to granite. He glared at her for a long moment, then looked away without answering.

Jonathan was torpid but conscious. Looking past Veronica to his father, he mumbled, "I wouldn't let *you* die, Pa! Not even if it meant I would be arrested and put in prison."

Anger flared in the big man. Leaping to his feet, he spit a brown stream of tobacco juice and walked to his prostrate son. Looking down at him, he grunted, "You ain't gonna die, kid! You know how females are. They always overreact to everything. You're gonna be okay. You get some rest today and tonight, and we'll get you to Buffalo tomorrow. The doc there will fix you up good—and he don't know us."

Jonathan shook his head in protest, and fear was written on his puffy face. "She says I'm bleedin' to death, Pa, and I think she's right! If you don't do somethin', I won't be alive tomorrow!"

"You will, too!" shouted Gordo. "I'm your pa! Would I lie to you? Would I let my own flesh and blood die? Huh? Would I?"

Jonathan did not answer.

The elder Silcox glared hotly at Veronica and spat, "No more of this 'Jonathan's gonna die' stuff. You hear me? You just keep workin' on that wound and get the bleedin' stopped!"

Veronica was about to respond when hoofbeats sounded

outside the barn. Drawing his gun, the buffalo hunter hurried to the big door, inched it open, and peered out. When he immediately holstered the gun, Veronica knew the rider was George Lang, returning from Dry Creek.

Silcox pulled the door open wider, and Lang dragged his horse inside. From the look on his face it was obvious that he was fearful and worried. "What's the matter?" the giant asked.

Lang answered, "Let me put my horse back with the others, then I'll tell you all about it."

As the tall, thin man led his horse to the stalls at the rear of the barn, Silcox snapped at his cohort, "I don't see no sacks! Where's the food? Didn't you get any whiskey?"

"I said I'll explain in a minute," Lang barked.

The giant eyed Veronica. "Somethin's wrong for sure. Maybe he's seen your boyfriend. If that's the case, you'd better say your prayers for him, 'cause his life's about over."

Veronica turned away, not knowing whether to feel fearful or relieved. Still, her heart began to beat faster, and she was most eager to hear what Lang had to say.

The feral-looking killer recrossed the barn with his hat off, sleeving sweat from his brow. Looking at Silcox, Lang told him, "It's that guy Cougar. He was in Dry Creek."

Silcox swore. "Did he see you?"

"No, but I sure saw him."

"So he's followin' us." Silcox turned and scowled at Veronica. "You prayin', girl?"

The young woman did not comment.

The massive buffalo hunter turned back to Lang and asked, "That why you didn't bring no food or whiskey?"

"Yeah. No time to get 'em." Sweat popped out on Lang's brow again, and he said with conviction, "Gordo, I'm tellin' you, this Cougar is no man to mess with. What he did to us in the Yellow Rose was nothin' compared to what he just did to three tough-lookin' hombres. He threw his knife thirty feet and stuck it in one of 'em's throat, and then he slammed another one's head against the bar over and over till he died. He left the third guy sprawled out on the floor, colder'n a mackerel."

Lang's words were faster and more anxious the more he spoke. "I tell you, Gordo, he ain't no ordinary lawman! We gotta get outta here! There ain't no way we're gonna be able to ambush him! The guy's almost not human! He'll keep after us and hunt us down and kill us, just like he killed them fellas at Dry Creek! Gordo, we gotta keep movin'. We gotta—"

"Get ahold of yourself!" cut in Silcox. "Cougar ain't gonna kill us. You're forgettin' somethin', ain't you?" He grinned evilly, then gestured at Veronica. "We got his woman!"

Veronica suddenly realized that she might be able to use Jonathan's fear of dying and Lang's fear of their pursuer to work them against Silcox—and Will Hardin would find them easier to conquer, divided. Standing up and stepping close to Gordo Silcox, she looked him square in the eye and said, "Your friend is right. My man is super-human. You got the drop on him at the Welton place simply by pure luck—and you won't always be that lucky. He'll find a way to get both you and Mr. Lang in spite of the fact that you have me. And remember something: Those men in the saloon in Dry Creek were not his parents' killers. If Cougar was that rough on *them*, just think what he'll do to you, your son, and your friend when he finds you!"

From the corner of her eye Veronica could see that what she was saying was having its effect on Lang. Looking back at Silcox, the blonde went on, "Of course, Cougar won't have to kill Jonathan. No . . . he's going to die shortly anyway because you won't get him to a doctor. And you'll have to live with that on your conscience—that is, if you have one."

While the younger Silcox lay pleading with his father to take him to Fort Kearney, George Lang stepped beside

Veronica, his ratlike face shiny with sweat, and choked, "Gordo, she's right! We're no match for Cougar! But if we surrender to him, maybe he'll have mercy and not kill us! Maybe if we give his woman back to him, he'll see that we get life in prison rather than a rope! Let's take Jonathan to the doctor at the fort, and if the lawman shows up there, we'll surrender! It's better than dyin', Gordo! It's a *whole* lot better than d—"

Gordo's big fist lashed out and caught Lang flush on the hollow of his jaw, and the impact of the blow sent the skinny man rolling across the earthen floor until he slammed against a feed bin and lay flat on his back. Silcox stomped after him and stood over him, breathing hotly with rage. Tobacco juice ran from the corner of his mouth as he bellowed, "Don't you ever let me hear that kind of talk come outta you again, George! We ain't surrenderin' to no tinhorn lawman! I'll get the drop on Cougar—and I'll kill him deader'n a doornail!"

Wheeling about, Silcox left Lang to regain his senses and stormed toward Veronica. She knew that an onslaught was coming, and she braced herself and lifted her chin, meeting his furious gaze.

Pointing a stiff finger at her, the giant sprayed her with brown saliva as he blared, "You keep your mouth shut, girl! I don't wanna hear no more outta you, you got that? Not nothin' about your boyfriend gettin' the better of us and not nothin' about my kid dyin'!"

The blonde pressed her lips tight and nodded, but she showed him no fear—and the defiant look in her eyes infuriated the huge man. Reaching out, he grabbed her by the hair and pulled her face so close she could smell his fetid breath. "I asked you if you got that!"

Though her hair felt as if it were going to come out by the roots, Veronica endured the pain without visibly flinching. Barely parting her lips, she answered simply, "Yes."

"See that you don't forget it!" Silcox snapped, and he shoved her roughly away. "Now, go tend to my son."

Just knowing that Lang had seen Cougar at Dry Creek was enough to instill courage and hope in Veronica Simmons. She also felt that she had succeeded in driving a wedge between Lang and Silcox, which she hoped would weaken their alliance. Turning away slowly, she went to Jonathan and sat down beside him, and as she looked at him, she realized that the younger Silcox would soon be dead. She was sure of it. What she did not know was what would happen to her then.

Suddenly a gunshot sounded from somewhere in the woods nearby. Lang leapt to his feet, throwing up his hands, and gasped, "It's him! It's him, Gordo! He's here! That lawman's here to kill us!"

Silcox swore and went toward the big door, saying, "Don't be stupid, George! It ain't Cougar; it's just a hunter. The lawman wouldn't give himself away by firin' a gun!"

Lang scurried across the barn and came up behind Silcox as the giant cautiously opened the door a few inches, the rusty hinges squeaking in protest. Peering around Silcox, he asked, "See anything?"

"Naw. Like I said . . . it's just a hunter."

Satisfied that Luke Bascomb had definitely gone, Marshal Will Hardin left his horse tied to a sapling, and then he took Deputy and crept cautiously through the dense forest toward the dilapidated barn that Cougar was sure the killers were holed up in. The dog seemed to understand that caution was necessary, and it stayed a few feet behind its new master at all times.

Hunkering behind some bushes about fifty yards from the barn, Cougar pulled Deputy down beside him. He put an arm around the dog and hugged it gently, whispering, "Ronnie's in that barn, boy, and we've got to get her out without endangering her life. I have to remember what Grandpa taught me—to be patient. So the first thing we're going to do is make a wide circle and take a look at the place from every side. It'll help us if we know the layout.

We've got to go at this very carefully; in fact, we'll probably have to wait till they come out. But we'll see."

As the day wore on, the marshal and his big furry
companion threaded their way through the woods, and
Cougar studied the area diligently. Soon they were back
where they had started. Although there was no sign of life,
he was sure that the buffalo hunters were hiding out in the
barn for one very good reason—Jonathan Silcox's poor
condition.

Certain that the travelers would be in there for quite
some time, Cougar went to his horse and pulled hardtack
and beef jerky from a saddlebag, as well as his canteen,
then returned to his post. The dog was still sitting and
watching the barn, and Hardin smiled to himself, thinking
that he would be hard pressed to find such an alert and
attentive human partner. He and Deputy ate until they
were full, and then he poured water into his hat and let
the dog drink from it while he drank from the canteen.

When darkness fell, the marshal patted his dog and
said, "Looks like we're going to be here for the night. I'd
like to just barge in there and end this whole thing in a
hurry, but I've already made one mistake like that, and I
can't afford another one. As much as it goes against my
grain, I'm going to follow Grandpa's advice."

Moonlight filtered into the big barn through cracks in
the walls and holes in the roof where shingles were missing. George Lang sat on the floor near the big door, which
was braced open a few inches, clutching a rifle and listening for any strange sounds. He peered through the opening into the forest, where the moon cast eerie shadows,
and at times Lang thought he saw the form of a man
moving beneath the trees. Each time, his heart would
pound violently as he focused on the form; then he would
see that it was only a shadow caused by the moving
branches.

At one point Lang thought he heard a scraping sound
somewhere inside the barn. His head whipped around and

he began to scan the dark interior. Quietly rising to his feet, feeling his pulse throbbing on the sides of his neck, he held the rifle ready and let his eyes roam the place. All was quiet except for the breathing of his sleeping companions.

Suddenly the scraping noise came again. Lang tensed, gripping the rifle with trembling hands. Where was it coming from? The hayloft? There was a door to the outside in the hayloft, and an old haywagon was parked next to the building outside with several wooden crates stacked on it. Hardin could climb onto those crates and enter the barn through that door!

Raising his eyes, he squinted at the hazy shadows up in the loft. For a moment he thought he saw movement. Blinking, he squinted harder, while his heart slammed his rib cage violently, making it difficult to get his breath. Something seemed to drift across the loft . . . a dark, nebulous shape that appeared to be moving toward the ladder that connected the barn floor with the loft.

Horror gripped the buffalo hunter. He was sure Will Hardin was in the loft and was moving stealthily toward the ladder so he could climb down and take Silcox and him by surprise. He must act now! Aiming the rifle muzzle at the loft, Lang searched for the moving shadow so he could draw a bead on it, but it was not there. Now he was certain Hardin had seen him and had ducked down.

The terrified buffalo hunter could stand it no longer. Racing over to his sleeping cohort, Lang drew a shuddering breath and whispered urgently, "Gordo! Gordo! Wake up! Hardin's here in the barn! He's come to kill us!"

Gordo Silcox woke immediately and scrambled to his feet. Revolver in hand, Silcox looked back and forth, saying, "Where is he, George?"

"Up in the loft!" Lang replied, dashing to stand beside the giant.

Silcox peered speculatively toward the loft. "Did you see him?"

"Well, not exactly. I . . . I mean I saw a shadow . . . I think."

"You *think*? Did you or didn't you?"

"Well, I heard a scrapin' sound. And then—"

Abruptly the scraping noise occurred again. "There! That's it!" Lang gasped. "Came from the loft, didn't it?"

"No, it didn't," Silcox said disgustedly. "It came from the back, where the horses are."

"Oh," Lang said weakly. "I'd swear it came from the loft."

"Where'd you see this shadow?"

"Up in the loft," replied Lang, using his rifle to point. "It was movin' from over there right toward the ladder."

"Did you *hear* anything?"

"Not when it was movin'."

Silcox swore, stomping a heavy foot. "George, you're spooked! You're lettin' your imagination get to you! Don't you know that loft floor is covered with dry hay and them boards are old and warped? There ain't no way a man could walk up there and not make plenty of noise. You're gonna have to get ahold of yourself."

Gordo Silcox looked over to where Jonathan and Veronica were lying. Veronica stirred restlessly, but Jonathan did not seem to be moving at all. Silcox walked over to his son, bent down, and put his finger on Jonathan's neck—and realized with horror and resignation that his son was dead.

Dawn came with a stiff wind whipping through the forest. When Will Hardin awakened and opened his eyes, Deputy was standing over him. The marshal roughed the scruff of the dog's neck and bid him good morning, then rose to his feet, put on his hat, and looked through the woods toward the barn. What he saw gave him a start. The big barn door was open and swinging loose in the wind.

A tingling sensation washed over Cougar's scalp. The killers had left with Veronica sometime during the night!

Hardin dashed toward the barn with the dog at his heels. When he was within thirty feet of the old structure, he drew up behind a tree and pulled his revolver. "Okay, Deputy," he whispered, "we go in nice and slow, just in case it's some kind of trap."

Moments later Hardin stood over the body of Jonathan Silcox where it lay on the barn floor. Breathing slowly, Cougar thought of Obadiah and murmured, "Well, Pa, chalk yourself up another one."

The dog sniffed at the corpse, then whined. "He's dead, all right, boy," said Cougar. "Guess his pa left his body here to rot." He shook his head. They must've moved real quietlike when they went. Even you didn't hear them, did you? If you had, you would have let me know."

Hardin glanced at the front of the barn, where the big door still swung in the wind, and announced, "Sun's coming up, Deputy. Let's you and me grab some breakfast from the saddlebags, then get on their trail. They'll move a lot faster now, without Jonathan."

Abruptly Deputy stared at the open doorway and stiffened, hackles rising. He began growling ferociously, then charged outside. "Hey, boy!" Cougar shouted. "What is it?"

The lawman started toward the door, but suddenly it slammed shut, the latch dropping into place. Whether it had closed from the wind or the hand of man, Cougar did not know, but he immediately drew his gun. Halfway to the door, he could hear the dog growling and snapping angrily when suddenly a gunshot cut the air and a man briefly howled. Cougar cocked the hammer of his Colt .45 and took another step, then a second shot rang out, this time from behind him, and a slug chewed into the floor near his feet.

Hardin whirled around, gun ready, and froze. Two men, their guns trained on him, were standing in the hayloft, silhouetted against the light of the open door behind them. One of the men shifted slightly, and the light fell on his face—the slashed-up face of Luke Bascomb. It was stitched in many places and covered with iodine and salve, making the wounds inflicted by the dog even more gruesome looking.

Deputy was still snapping and snarling fiercely outside, but Bascomb disregarded the commotion, shouting, "You didn't really think I'd just let it go, did you, lawman? You shamed me and killed my friends in Dry Creek, and your ugly hound almost chewed me to pieces. So I brought three more of my friends with me. Two of them are out there about to kill your mutt. Seems they missed with that first shot, but he'll be one dead dog in a minute. We're gonna wait right here till he is, then I'm gonna have me some fun killin' you an inch at a time."

When Deputy plunged through the door, he saw a man to his right bringing a gun to bear. Then the barn door slammed, and the dog turned to see a second man holding a gun on him. Lunging with blinding speed at the man closest to him, Deputy went for the man's gun hand. When his fangs closed on the man's wrist, the cocked gun fired prematurely, and instead of hitting the dog, the slug tore into the other man's chest, killing him.

The man the dog had attacked went down under his weight. Saliva sprayed and blood ran as the huge beast's razor-sharp fangs ripped into the man's jugulars. The victim tried to scream, but Deputy tore his throat open and cut off the scream before it was born. When the man breathed out his last breath and went limp, the black dog stood over him, gave a snarl of triumph, then turned to look at the other assailant. But the man lay still, his sightless eyes staring toward the brightening sky.

Knowing its master was inside the barn, the huge black dog dashed to the door and began to bark and scratch wildly. He relentlessly clawed the rotting wood with his sharp nails, desperately trying to gain entry.

Luke Bascomb's lacerated face showed concern at the dog's continued growling. Holding his gun steady on the marshal below, he told his cohort, "Art, go see what's happenin' out there. I don't like the sound of it."

Just as Art turned to comply, Deputy leapt against the outside of the door, barking and scratching furiously. Both men shifted their eyes off Hardin for a brief moment—just long enough for him to dart across the floor. They both immediately fired at him, but it was too late, for he had plunged underneath the hayloft and began shooting up at them through the floorboards. Cursing loudly, the men scrambled around, attempting to evade the bullets while firing back.

Suddenly Bascomb's partner took a slug under the chin that tore through the top of his head. Mortally wounded, he fell hard, slamming onto the floor. Cougar kept firing until his gun was empty, but his last bullet plowed through Bascomb's right foot. The drifter bellowed with pain, staggered momentarily, then fired *his* last shot through the floor. But Cougar had flattened himself up against the wall, and the slug missed him by four feet. When he heard Bascomb's hammer strike an empty cartridge, instead of reloading, he holstered his Colt .45 and dashed for the ladder. He would take the drifter with his bare hands.

Up in the loft, the wounded Bascomb started to reload, then heard the lawman coming after him. He jammed his empty gun in its holster and limped toward the door by which he and his cohort had entered, but as Bascomb reached the open loft door, his expression turned from fear to horror. The huge black dog was adeptly climbing the crates on the old haywagon and coming at him, its eyes blazing and its lips curled back, exposing the gleaming fangs. The drifter suddenly seemed paralyzed.

His teeth snapping, Deputy bounded through the loft door and attacked the terrified man, and the impact of the dog's one hundred and fifty pounds sent Bascomb reeling backward. Cougar was halfway up the ladder when Luke Bascomb's body sailed past him and flew off the edge of the loft onto the barn floor. Right behind him was the snarling, slavering dog.

The drifter's eyes bulged with terror as the mass of black fur lunged at him. The last sound Luke Bascomb ever made was a scream.

Chapter Eleven

Several days after leaving the barn, Gordo Silcox, George Lang, and their hostage traveled through the eastern foothills of the Laramie Mountains in southern Wyoming. As she rode between her captors on Jonathan Silcox's horse, Veronica Simmons thought that at least her knee was giving her less pain, and the swelling had finally subsided a great deal.

Lang cast a glance at the setting sun and said, "Gordo, I'm really hungry. What say we push on down to La Bonte and get us a good meal at that café we ate at once?"

"Naw, I don't want to go into no towns till we're free of Cougar," growled Silcox. "I don't want Veronica's boyfriend to catch up to us when there are people around he could enlist to help him take us." He scratched his neck, which had gotten even grimier, and said, "Instead of goin' into La Bonte for a meal, we'll find us a small ranch around here. You know, one that ain't big enough to have hired hands. Kinda like at the Weltons." He laughed, adding, "We'll tell a real good story and get us a free supper tonight and a free breakfast in the mornin'. Maybe even a nice bed to sleep in."

Veronica had no doubt that Will Hardin was still following and was being very cautious because of Silcox's threat to shoot her. She thought of her parents and tried to imagine the kind of torture they were experiencing. All they could do was pray and wait.

The sun dropped behind the Laramie Mountains, turning the foothills a deep purple. The travelers caught a glimpse of the town of La Bonte a few miles off to the left, and then Silcox pointed to a small ranch in a shallow valley just ahead. "That place'll be perfect," he announced. "That's where we'll spend the night."

A small herd of cattle dotted the green pasture behind the ranch house and outbuildings. Periodically a calf cried for its mother, and within seconds a reassuring bawling answer came. As the riders drew near the buildings, they saw a couple sitting on the front porch of the house. The rancher and his wife, in turn, had obviously spotted them and were watching their approach.

Speaking softly, Silcox warned Veronica, "Same goes here as at the Weltons, girlie. You let on that you're our prisoner, and those people will die in front of your eyes. So let me do the talkin', and you just agree with everythin' I say. Got it?"

"Yes," Veronica replied stiffly. "Just don't hurt them. Please."

Shrugging, the giant said, "It's up to you. You keep your trap shut, and everything'll be fine."

The rancher and his wife, who appeared to be in their early thirties, stood and walked to the edge of their porch as the three riders came into the yard. As Wyoming's population was small, sometimes days would pass without ranchers such as these seeing another human being. Travelers passing through were always welcome—although when the couple looked more closely at the two unkempt men in the dim light of the dying day, it was apparent from their faces that they felt a touch of discomfort. However, Veronica's presence seemed to make her companions acceptable to the rancher and his wife.

"Hello!" said the rancher, nodding with a smile.

"Howdy," Gordo Silcox responded as the three horses came to a halt. "We're travelin' through on our way down to New Mexico, and we was wonderin' if you folks might have an extra bed or two that we could rent from you. We've been on the trail for several days, and my niece here has a banged-up knee and could use a good night's rest."

"We've only got one extra bed," replied the rancher, "but she's welcome to it without any charge. As for you gentlemen, we have a back porch with plenty of floor space. If you wouldn't mind sleeping there, my wife can supply you with blankets and pillows."

"That'd be just fine," the huge man declared expansively, grinning with pleasure. "By the way, my name's Gordo Silcox, and this here's my partner, George Lang. My niece is Veronica Simmons."

"I'm Martin Tolliver," the rancher said, "and this is my wife, Harriet. Climb down and come on in. Harriet was just about to begin preparing supper, and you folks are welcome to join us."

"Much obliged," Silcox said with feeling. The two men dismounted quickly, but because of her bad knee, Veronica took her time getting down from her horse. Martin Tolliver hurried off the porch, saying, "Here, Miss Simmons, let me help you."

"Thank you," replied the young blonde, allowing the rancher to take her by the upper arms and lower her gently to the ground.

Harriet Tolliver stepped beside Veronica, suggesting, "Let me get on one side and my husband on the other, and we'll help you into the house."

"Oh, that won't be necessary," Veronica said, steadying herself. "I can walk." She gave them a small smile, adding, "It just takes me a little longer to get where I'm going."

Frowning with concern, Harriet asked, "How did you hurt yourself?"

Before Veronica could answer, Silcox butted in. "Her horse shied on her up north. Threw her off. Had the doc at Buffalo look it over, and he said it's sprained mighty bad, but she'll be okay."

The buffalo hunters followed closely as the Tollivers escorted Veronica into the house. The hallway passed the parlor and ended in the kitchen, a large room with a big round table surrounded by straight-backed chairs. Once in close quarters, the stench of the buffalo hunters' bodies became extremely apparent, and the Tollivers gave each other a furtive look, then shrugged.

The guests were seated, and the rancher started a fire in the cookstove while his wife began peeling potatoes. Veronica offered to help prepare the meal, and although Harriet refused at first, she relented when Veronica insisted that she could peel the potatoes sitting down.

While Harriet was working at the counter by the sink, she said to Veronica, "It's a shame you have to travel with your knee so badly sprained. Couldn't the trip have been postponed until it healed?"

Veronica cast a quick glance toward Silcox before answering—a look that the rancher's wife clearly noticed. The huge man spoke up. "It's like this, Mrs. Tolliver. Veronica's parents—my sister and her husband—were killed by Indians a couple weeks ago up near Buffalo, just before me and my partner happened to be comin' for a visit. Veronica don't have no one else to look to, so I offered to take her to my home down near Santa Fe. Unfortunately I got some pressin' business and have to get back, so there weren't no choice about her ridin' with that bum leg."

Harriet nodded and looked at Veronica. The school-teacher did not meet her gaze, but rather busied herself with the potatoes. Speaking softly, the rancher's wife told her young guest, "I'm so sorry. Please accept my condolences."

Without looking up, Veronica responded, "Thank you, Mrs. Tolliver."

Martin Tolliver asked Silcox, "Was it Cheyenne that killed your sister and brother-in-law?"

"Uh . . . yeah. Yeah. It was Cheyenne."

"Renegades?"

"Huh?"

"Renegades. You know . . . who jumped one of the reservations."

George Lang quickly replied, "Yeah, that's right. We talked to some soldiers from Fort Kearney, and they said the redskins what killed Veronica's ma and pa had left the Wind River reservation."

"We've had some problems in these parts, too," remarked Tolliver. "There's a renegade band of Cheyenne riding about, causing trouble. The leader's a chief's son named Black Shirt. He's a bad sort. Hates whites."

"He don't hate whites as much as I hate Indians," grunted Silcox.

"Why's that?" queried Tolliver.

The buffalo hunter jutted his jaw. "The way they torture white men, that's why. Hangin' 'em upside down by their ankles and cuttin' 'em to ribbons a little at a time for days before they die. Or tyin' 'em to a tree and burnin' 'em to death with red-hot irons. Or cookin' 'em over hot coals like you'd roast a hog. Dirty heathens! If I had my way, us white folks would execute every last one of 'em."

"I hear tell this Black Shirt has some tortures worse than those," Tolliver observed. "I sure wouldn't want him mad at me."

Silcox shook his head angrily. "The Army oughtta ride him down and cut his head off," he mumbled. "Stinkin' redskins ain't got no right to treat white folks like they do."

"They think they have," spoke up Harriet. "And while I agree that their tortures are barbarous, they're only doing to us what we would do to them if the tables were turned."

"What do you mean by that?" Silcox asked, staring at the woman.

"What would *you* do if your ancestors had owned this land for thousands of years, and suddenly men came in and stole it from you, then stripped you of your dignity by penning you up on a reservation like some kind of animal? Wouldn't you retaliate?"

Silcox fixed the woman with his small piglike eyes and

replied levelly, "You bet I'd retaliate, lady—but I'd just kill 'em flat out. I wouldn't torture 'em."

Veronica lifted her head and gave the man a dry look, then returned to her chore.

An uncomfortable silence fell over the room. Changing the subject, Martin Tolliver turned to George Lang and commented, "Looks like you got your face burned pretty bad, Mr. Lang. How'd it happen?"

Lang looked for a moment at Veronica, who did not meet his gaze. After flicking a glance at Silcox, he replied to the rancher, "This thing's been a nightmare to me, Mr. Tolliver. I'd rather not talk about it."

"Sure," Tolliver murmured. "Sorry. I was just making conversation. Didn't mean to pry."

"No harm done," responded the skinny man.

Again a weighty silence descended.

"Tell you what, gentlemen," Harriet declared brightly. "Why don't you all go out to the well and get washed up? If you take your time, Miss Simmons and I will be just about ready to feed you when you return."

The schoolteacher smiled at her hostess, saying, "Please call me Veronica."

"All right." She smiled, reiterating, "As I was saying, Veronica and I will be ready to feed you hungry men when you return."

Gordo Silcox looked down at his filthy hands, then stared at the rancher's wife. It was obvious that the idea was a strange one to him, unaccustomed as he was to washing his hands before a meal. He then looked sharply at Veronica, and his intention was clear: He did not like the idea of leaving her alone with Harriet Tolliver. But as Martin Tolliver was already urging George Lang toward the back door, Silcox would have to go along. He gave the young blonde a warning look, then followed the others.

Tolliver stepped onto the porch and lit a lantern, then headed toward the barn. "Where's the well?" asked Lang as he followed alongside the rancher. "In the barn?"

"No," Tolliver replied, chuckling. "It's behind the tool-shed, next to the barn."

The toolshed, which stood roughly fifty feet from the house, was a fairly new structure with a peaked roof, windows in the sides, and a door facing the back of the house. Behind the toolshed was the circular well, and next to the well was a large, nearly full rain barrel. Beside it stood a small table that held a washbasin.

Tolliver lifted the basin and dipped it into the rain barrel. "No sense using the well water when we've got plenty in the barrel," he remarked. Holding out a bar of lye soap that had been left on the table, he amiably told the two scruffy buffalo hunters, "Okay, gentlemen. As my guests, you go first."

Gritting their teeth, the outlaws began scrubbing their hands.

Nearly fifteen minutes had passed by the time the men returned to the house. The women had done little talking while they were alone, although several meaningful looks had passed between them. Both Veronica and Harriet were relatively quiet during the meal, while the men discussed various subjects. When supper was over, Martin Tolliver suggested, "Since you folks have been on the trail for a while, I'm sure you'd like to bathe."

Harriet concurred, "I'm sure they would. And Martin, since you men will be bathing at the rain barrel, why don't you bring some water in here, and Veronica and I will bathe here in the kitchen."

Veronica had noticed the big galvanized tub on the back porch. "Oh! That would be wonderful!" she exclaimed.

Gordo Silcox and George Lang exchanged glances, and it was apparent that the idea of a bath was repugnant to them. Lang protested, "Well, that ain't really necessary, folks. Right, Gordo?"

Silcox stared for a long moment at Veronica, as he was clearly not eager to leave his captive alone again with the rancher's wife—and even less keen to wash his foul-smelling body. However, he reluctantly agreed, saying, "Well, now,

George, we're civilized men . . . as my niece can attest. So let's help Mr. Tolliver carry in some water for the ladies. Then we'll take our baths and wash some of this trail dust off of us."

Lang's face fell with disappointment, but there was nothing he could say or do that would save him from his ghastly fate without making it all too plain that Veronica Simmons was in no way related to Gordo Silcox.

After bringing the tub into the kitchen, Tolliver carried two metal buckets out to the well. He and Silcox made several trips, slowly filling up the big tub. The last two bucketsful were left in their containers and placed on the stove to heat. As the men were leaving to take their baths, Silcox caught Veronica's eye and gave her a threatening look. She understood it all too well: These kind and congenial people would be murdered it she revealed the truth to either of them.

After the women had finished bathing, Harriet loaned Veronica a nightgown and robe to wear while they washed the young woman's clothes. Standing by the sink, Harriet removed her hands from the soapy water and turned toward her guest, looking her squarely in the eye. "Veronica . . ." she said softly.

"Yes?"

"I want to ask you something—and if I'm probing where I don't belong, you just say so, okay?"

Veronica dropped her eyes, knowing what was coming. The woman suspected something. "All right."

"Are you in some kind of trouble?"

"Why, no," lied the blonde, forcing a note of surprise into her voice. "What makes you think that?"

"I . . . well, I see fear in your eyes. And you seem quite on edge."

Veronica's fear was for the Tollivers. Her own life was not in danger as long as Gordo Silcox needed her as a hostage. Tight-lipped and cautious, she lied again. Giving Harriet a weak smile, she allowed, "It must be the pain in my knee and the weariness from traveling that make me look distressed. I assure you, I'm not in trouble, and I'm really not on edge."

Harriet peered intently at the young woman but said no more. With a sigh she turned back to the sink.

Veronica's clothes were hung up to dry, and when the men returned, Silcox cast a wary eye at the schoolteacher. She gave him a bland look, as if to say, "Your secret is still safe." She was then escorted to her room by Harriet, while her captors put the horses in the corral and bedded down on the back porch.

Crickets played their music and a partial moon bathed the yard with its pale silver light. As the buffalo hunters lay on the porch, George Lang raised his head and ran a nervous gaze over the panorama. "Maybe one of us oughtta stay awake, Gordo. I've been expectin' Hardin to show up at any time."

"I was about to suggest that myself," Silcox responded, yawning. "You seem more awake than me. How about you takin' the first watch?"

"Okay. I'll wake you in a couple hours. We can trade off till dawn." Sitting up, the cadaverous-looking killer leaned against a post. After a few seconds he asked, "Gordo, do you feel funny?"

"What do you mean?" came the dull response.

"My clothes keep stickin' to me."

"Oh, that. Yeah. Me, too. It's 'cause the crust we had on our skin is gone. Don't know why folks want to wash so often. Plenty uncomfortable, ain't it?"

"Sure is. I can't wait to get back to normal again."

"It won't take long," Silcox assured him, then dropped off to sleep.

Alone with her husband as they lay in bed, Harriet Tolliver watched the night breeze toying with the curtains at their bedroom windows. After a few minutes she turned to Martin and asked quietly, "Honey, do you get the feeling that Veronica is afraid of something?"

"Yep. I'd bet on it. I've been thinking about it, but I don't know what to do. I hate to stick my nose in other people's business."

"While you men were bathing I asked her if she was in trouble."

"What'd she say?"

"Said nothing was wrong, and she tried to make me think I was misreading her. But I know I'm not. If she were really traveling with her uncle like we're supposed to believe, she'd have brought some clothing—but she has only what she was wearing when they rode in here." Harriet was silent for a moment, then added, "I've got a feeling that that horrid-looking huge man isn't her uncle at all."

"I was thinking the same thing," Martin remarked. "In fact, my feeling is that she's possibly being held captive." The rancher squeezed his wife's hand. "I'll find out the truth in the morning by bluffing those two repulsive-looking characters. If they *are* holding Veronica against her will—"

"Oh, Martin!" gasped Harriet, gripping his arm. "Please be careful! By the looks of them, I think they could be extremely violent men!"

"I'll be careful, honey," Martin responded soothingly, "but if those two *have* abducted her, we sure can't let them leave here with her."

Lying on her bed in the darkness, Veronica Simmons considered her plight. She was sure that Cougar Will Hardin had not rescued her yet because the circumstances had made it impossible and he would not risk getting her killed. Feeling a cool, refreshing breeze play over her face and arms, her eyes strayed to the open window across the room. For a moment she considered climbing out the window and running as fast and as far as she could, but she quickly discarded the idea. Her escape would no doubt give the wicked buffalo hunters cause to murder the Tollivers. And she could not get very far before they

tracked her down. Gordo Silcox undoubtedly knew she
was smart enough to figure that out—and that was why he
could sleep outside without worry.

The young schoolteacher reflected again on Will Hardin.
Hearing his last words over and over, the beautiful blonde
fought back tears as she realized that he had fallen in love
with her—what she had prayed for and dreamed of for so
long.

Dismal thoughts abruptly forced their way into Veronica's mind. What if something had happened to Cougar?
Maybe he had not come because he *could* not come!
Maybe he would *never* come! And if he did not show up
after a reasonable amount of time, they would figure he
was not coming. Sooner or later Silcox would kill her . . .
or worse.

Sleep eluded Veronica Simmons virtually the entire
night as she tossed and turned on the bed, wrestling with
the thoughts that tormented her.

Dawn was a few minutes old when Gordo Silcox and
George Lang stepped off the back porch and headed
toward the corral. Watching them from where he stood at
his bedroom window, Martin Tolliver heard the men say
they were going to bridle and saddle the horses to be
ready to leave immediately after breakfast.

Harriet, barely awake, raised up on her elbows and
asked her husband, "What are you doing?"

"Keeping an eye on Silcox and Lang," the rancher replied without turning to look at her. "They're planning on
riding out early."

Pivoting abruptly, Tolliver strode across the bedroom to
a wall peg and took down his gun belt that held a holstered
Colt .45 Peacemaker. As he was strapping the belt on, his
wife sat up, wide-eyed, and exclaimed, "Martin, what are
you doing?"

"I'm going to question those two at breakfast—and I
want to be prepared if I get the wrong answer."

"But they'll kill you!" she half-whispered, scurrying out

of bed and confronting him. "You're not a gunman, darling! You wouldn't stand a chance with those men! You weren't wearing a gun yesterday, so if they even see you wearing it today, it might be enough to start trouble. Please, take it off!"

Setting his jaw stubbornly, Martin Tolliver countered, "If that young woman is being held prisoner, I can't let them ride out of here with her, Harriet! Can't you see that?"

Harriet Tolliver's face was pale with fear. Her hands trembled as she gripped her husband's arms, and she told him, "Martin, I appreciate what you're trying to do for Veronica, but I don't want to see you get killed in the process! Please, I beg of you! Take off the gun!"

Tolliver studied Harriet's anguished eyes for a long moment, then sighed. "All right, honey. I'll take it off. But it's going to be where I can get to it in a hurry, if I have to. I can't let them take that poor young woman with them if what we're thinking is true."

"But getting yourself killed isn't the solution!" Harriet cried, running her fingers through her tousled brown hair. "Let's do it this way. Let them ride away, then we'll hurry into La Bonte and get the marshal. He can then get up a posse and go after Silcox and Lang. If Veronica is a captive, certainly she would speak up and say so once she had the protection of the marshal."

"All right," Tolliver agreed. "If it will make you feel better, we'll do it your way." As he spoke he replaced the gun belt on the wall peg.

A short while later the Tollivers and their guests sat down at the breakfast table, and it was evident to Veronica Simmons that the pale and withdrawn Harriet was quite nervous. Her hands trembled, and she avoided looking at Silcox and Lang, and when the giant asked for a cup of coffee, the coffeepot shook alarmingly in her hand, sloshing the liquid out of his cup.

The buffalo hunter abruptly swung his gaze from Har-

riet to Veronica, and his piercing stare wordlessly demanded of her, "Have you told the Tollivers the truth?"
Shaking her head slightly, the schoolteacher indicated that
she had not revealed anything—and she prayed that he
believed her.

Veronica felt Martin Tolliver watching her, and she
flicked her glance at him. Seeing the questioning look on
her host's face, she realized that he had seen the silent
exchange that had gone on between her and the killer . . .
and she also knew that he had guessed the truth: Veronica
was being held against her will.

She was about to say something to distract the rancher
when he looked at Silcox and blurted angrily, "You're not
really Veronica's uncle, are you?"

The coffeepot slipped from Harriet's hand, spilling its
contents all over the table. George Lang's head jerked up,
and he stared at his cohort, who scowled menacingly at
Martin Tolliver and snapped, "Who told you that?"

"Veronica," the rancher replied, meaning that her actions and expressions had revealed it.

The blonde's mouth dropped open and her eyes wid-
ened. Shaking her head, she insisted, "No! I didn't say a
thing! Honestly!"

Silcox swore. Standing up and banging his fist on the
table, he roared, "You little fool! Now these people have
to die!"

"No!" Veronica screamed. "I didn't tell them! I swear it!
You've got to believe—"

The outlaw smacked her face with all his might, knocking her backward and tipping the chair over, dumping her
on the floor.

Harriet screamed, and infuriated, Martin Tolliver leapt
to his feet and jumped Silcox, but the giant shook him off
easily, then swung a meaty fist into the rancher's mouth,
smashing Tolliver's lips against his teeth. Screaming again,
Harriet grabbed an iron skillet from the stove and raced
for Silcox, but George Lang saw her and lunged for the
woman, seizing her wrist. Twisting it hard, he made her

drop the skillet, then held the wriggling woman tightly in his grasp, keeping her from going after Silcox again.

Ignoring the pain from both the blow and her knee, which had been severely wrenched, Veronica started crawling toward the cupboard. While watching Harriet clean up the kitchen the night before, Veronica had seen that a carving knife was kept in the top drawer—and she also knew that unless she could do something to prevent it, the Tollivers would be murdered.

Martin Tolliver and Gordo Silcox were in a clinch as they fought near the back door. The buffalo hunter tried to use his advantage in size to slam the rancher against the doorjamb, but Tolliver ducked and slipped away from him. The giant came at him, but Tolliver ducked the huge fist and countered by punching the outlaw hard on the temple. Before Silcox recovered, the rancher punched him again, this time on the jaw.

Cursing loudly, rage evident in his narrow-set, beady eyes, a furious Gordo Silcox abruptly pulled his revolver and aimed it at the rancher's head. Tolliver stared in horror as Silcox thumbed back the hammer, grinning wickedly, then pulled the trigger. The gun roared, sending the slug through Martin Tolliver's head.

Harriet Tolliver shrieked with agony, screaming her husband's name. With a burst of strength she wrenched herself free of George Lang's grip and lunged for Gordo Silcox, leaping onto his back and trying to scratch the giant's eyes out. The huge man howled, staggering about with Harriet hanging on to him. Holstering his gun, he reached back, pulled her off, and threw her against a wall.

Still screaming, the crazed woman scrambled to her feet, ready to attack Silcox again, but George Lang whipped out his gun and shot her in the chest. The bullet ripped through her heart, killing her instantly.

As Harriet's body tumbled to the floor, Veronica managed to wrench open the drawer and grab hold of the knife, hoping to plunge it into George Lang's back. But

Gordo Silcox saw her and, drawing his revolver, roared, "Drop it!"

Silcox's shout checked her, and she stared at the ominous black muzzle of his revolver for a moment, then let the carving knife fall to the floor. Looking at the sprawled bodies of Martin and Harriet Tolliver, the young woman began to weep. The gallant pair had figured out that she was in danger, and they had lost their lives trying to help her.

Color crept into George Lang's feral face, and his eyes blazed as he picked up the knife and glared at Veronica. Waving the blade threateningly in her face, he spat, "You were gonna stab me with this, weren't you?"

Veronica glared at him and answered heatedly, "Yes, I was going to stab you! I'd kill you both if I could, you filthy murderers!" Before she could say anything more, Silcox seized her by the arm and flung her onto a chair by the kitchen table, and she winced as pain shot through her knee.

Lang threw the carving knife onto the counter and demanded of his cohort, "Gordo, we gotta get outta here! Cougar could show up at any time!"

Silcox shook his head stubbornly and replied, "We ain't goin' nowhere. I'm tired of runnin'. We're waitin' right here, and then you and me are gonna kill him!"

The smaller man's face went chalky. "I'm tellin' you, when only two men are up against him, they're outnumbered!" Licking dry lips, Lang asked, "Have you forgotten how he handled the four of us in Sheridan? And weren't you listenin' when I told you what he did to those drifters at Dry Creek? I tell you, Gordo, he ain't like normal men. It's . . . it's like he's part beast! No wonder they call him Cougar!"

The rejoinder came spewing out of Silcox's mouth. "Even a cougar can be killed! We'll stay right where we are till that stinkin' lawman finds us. Don't forget, we got the advantage over him: We're inside—and we've got his woman." He regarded Veronica for a moment, then told

Lang, "After we kill him, I'll give you the privilege of takin' out vengeance on this female for throwin' boilin' water in your face. Now, c'mon. Let's take these bodies and throw 'em in the toolshed. I'm sick of lookin' at 'em."

The killers made Veronica follow along while they dragged the bodies of Martin and Harriet Tolliver across the yard and into the toolshed. As they were heading back to the house, one of the Tollivers' horses nickered in the corral by the barn. George Lang swung his head in that direction and pulled his gun. Breathing hard, he gasped, "He's in the barn, Gordo! Take cover!"

Silcox dropped his hand to the butt of his revolver as Lang ran into the house, and his own horse, which stood at the porch with Veronica's and Lang's, nickered back at the other horse. The big man locked an arm around the schoolteacher's neck and pointed the gun at her head. Staring toward the barn, he shouted, "Hardin! If you're in that barn, come out this instant, or I'll blow your girlfriend's brains out!"

The morning air was completely still, and not a sound was heard. Then another horse in the corral whinnied. Silcox pressed the gun tightly against Veronica's head and shouted once more for Cougar to show himself. After several silent minutes the killer grunted to Veronica, "He ain't in there. Let's go back in the house."

Entering the kitchen, Silcox said in a tone of disgust, "You're just jumpy, George. Hardin wasn't there. You gotta get ahold of yourself."

As Veronica dropped onto one of the kitchen chairs, Lang retorted, "What about you, Gordo? How come you pulled your gun? Seems to me you're jumpy, too!"

"It's just you puttin' me on edge!" snapped the giant. "Get a grip on yourself!"

Veronica glanced at George Lang, whose nerves were obviously stretched and frayed almost to the breaking point. A light sheen moistened his brow, and his hands shook. Looking at the gun clutched in his right hand, Veronica thought that he would be quite useless in a shoot-out, for there would be no way he could aim accurately. Panicking, Lang started past Silcox, who stood near the door, watching him closely.

The big man grabbed Lang's arm and rasped, "Where do you think you're goin'?"

"Outta here, that's where!" he shouted, jerking his arm loose. "If you want to stay and let that lawman kill you, that's your business . . . but I'm leavin'!"

Silcox seized his arm again. "You ain't goin' nowhere!"

Lang's fear of Cougar was clearly greater than his fear of Silcox, for he again yanked his arm free, cursing loudly. But the giant leapt in front of Lang, filling the doorway and blocking his exit. "I said you ain't leavin'!" Silcox snarled in a tone of finality.

Violence hung between them for a long, tense moment. Then Lang clawed for his gun, and in retaliation the giant's fist shot out and smashed into Lang's cheek. As the tall, thin man slipped to the floor, an enraged Silcox jumped on top of him and began pounding Lang's face with his huge fists.

Veronica's heart beat loudly against her ribs. This was her chance to escape, while the two men were battling each other. Taking a deep breath, the blonde stood and limped as quickly as she could across the kitchen and through the doorway. The pain in her knee was excruciating, but she gritted her teeth, stepped off the porch, and made her way to her horse. Gripping the saddle horn, she put her left foot in the stirrup and tried to raise herself up, but the horse was tall, making it difficult for someone her size to mount.

She strained to listen: The fight continued. Whimpering with anxiety, Veronica struggled to pull herself into the saddle. Just as she was about to swing her leg over, the nervous horse sidestepped, and the move caused Veronica to slip and come down on her bad leg.

Clinging to the saddle horn, she called upon her reserves of strength and finally hoisted herself onto the saddle. She managed to turn the animal around, but the frightened horse balked at going any farther, and she was screaming at the animal to obey her when she felt a powerful hand grip her waist. Her heart sank as Gordo Silcox yanked her from the saddle, swearing profusely. Veronica kicked and screamed, but it was to no avail, and the massive man carried her back inside the house and slammed her down on a chair. She yelped with pain, then buried her face in her hands and sobbed.

Silcox stood over her and spat, "*You* ain't goin' nowhere either, woman! Try that again and I'll beat you to a pulp, like I did George!"

While Veronica stayed slumped in the chair, weeping, Gordo Silcox clomped his way across the floor to the water pail in the sink. Carrying the pail to where George Lang lay semiconscious on the floor, he threw its contents in Lang's face.

Sputtering, Lang regained consciousness, and Silcox planted him on a chair and growled, "Do we have an understandin' now, pardner?"

Lang's burned and peeling skin was now bruised and bleeding. Dabbing at his face with his filthy bandanna, he choked, "Yeah. We have an understandin'."

"Good!" Silcox exclaimed, grinning. "That's much better. Now, as I was sayin', we've got the advantage over Cougar, and we've got his girl. No doubt about it. That lawman's comin' as sure as Monday follows Sunday—and we're gonna be ready for him."

Chapter Twelve

More than twenty four hours passed. At midmorning the following day, with a hot wind sweeping across the hills, Gordo Silcox and George Lang paced nervously inside the house, watching through all the windows. Veronica Simmons, her hair disheveled and her face moist with sweat, was tied to a chair in the kitchen, her hands lashed in front of her.

Lang was assigned to patrol the parlor and the two bedrooms. Periodic gusts of wind whipped through the open windows, fluttering the curtains, and the cadaverous-looking killer practically jumped out of his skin every time, certain that Will Hardin was climbing through.

Silcox stayed in the kitchen, moving from window to window and pausing at each to carefully study the view it allowed. The house was heating up, and the giant pulled off his hat and tossed it onto the kitchen table before going to the water pail and downing three full dippers. He then cautiously opened the back door and peered out, checking the horses, still saddled and tied near the back porch in case they had to ride away in a hurry. The wind ruffled the animals' manes, and a dust devil skipped across the yard, throwing dirt particles hard against the house. As the buffalo hunter gazed slowly around the area, he was satisfied that there was no movement other than what was caused by the wind.

When Silcox closed the door and wiped the sweat from his homely face, Veronica shifted to lessen the discomfort and said through parched lips, "I'm awfully thirsty. May I have a drink of water?"

Eyeing her with contempt, the huge killer grunted, "Why should I give you water? You said you'd kill me if you could."

Veronica responded bitterly, "I've watched you and your friend murder innocent people, you're determined to kill the man I love, and you've promised Lang that he can kill me after that. Am I supposed to look kindly on you?"

Silcox shrugged his broad shoulders. "Okay, so you got a right to hate my guts. But I'm still in charge, and I say you don't get no water."

With that, the giant walked back to the water pail and ran the ladle along the bottom. When he found it nearly empty, he picked up the bucket and drank directly from it, gulping loudly and spilling some water onto his shirt. Setting the bucket down, he belched, then wiped a sleeve across his mouth. Veronica's blue eyes bored into him as he resumed his vigil from window to window.

Presently George Lang entered the kitchen and headed for the water pail. He dipped the ladle in, and it came up empty. Then he peered inside. Turning to Silcox, who was now looking out the partly open back door, he said, "Gordo, the bucket's dry."

The big man threw Lang a dull glance and replied, "So? Whaddya want me to do about it?"

"Well, since you drank nearly all of it, I think you oughtta be the one to go to the well and get some more," Lang told him.

"That's what you get for thinkin' when you ain't used to it," the bearded giant mocked. "You want water, you go fetch it."

Scrubbing a hand over his sweaty, battered face, Lang swallowed hard, and his hands began to shake. He was clearly afraid to go out to the well alone. But the house was hot, and he needed a drink. With a sigh he resignedly picked up the pail, pushed past Silcox's massive frame, and stepped out into the heat of the day.

Lang took a deep breath and stepped off the porch, then headed toward the well behind the toolshed. A sudden gust of wind snatched the hat from his head and sent it sailing toward the barn. He started to go after it, then waved a dismissive hand at it as it bounced and cartwheeled to the far end of the yard. Seconds later he rounded the corner of the shed, out of sight of the house.

Lang approached the well warily, but after looking cautiously around, he picked up the rope and tied it to the handle of the pail. Lowering the pail down into the well, he watched it as it slowly filled.

Suddenly two strong hands seized Lang from behind. A palm was then clamped over his mouth as his neck was locked in the crook of a powerful arm, and the rope slipped from Lang's fingers, the pail falling into the well. A look of horror immediately spread over his face, and with his eyes bulging, the panic-stricken killer twisted enough to catch a glimpse of Will Hardin's scarred face.

Holding the killer in a viselike grip, Cougar hissed into his ear, "This was what I was waiting for, Lang! I knew sooner or later one of you'd come out without Veronica, and I could make my move!"

Lang tried desperately to wrestle free of the hand, but Hardin merely tightened his pressure on the man's neck. Then the buffalo hunter spotted the huge, snarling, mean-looking dog at the lawman's heels, and he began to whine, the sound escaping through his nose.

Hardin warned, "My dog is a man-killer, so if you so much as blink, he'll be on you faster than a snake's tongue, and he'll tear your Adam's apple out. Now, I'm going to take my hand off your mouth to handcuff you, and I'm warning you, don't make a sound. If you do, I'll be forced to kill you, Lang. Mind you, I'd be glad to give you your wish, but I'm a lawman—which means I'm supposed to

bring you back alive to stand trial . . . if possible. But if
you holler for Silcox, you're a dead man. Understand?"

Lang nodded.

The marshal had barely taken his hand away when Lang
drew a breath and started to yell. Hardin immediately
grabbed Lang by the throat with both hands, bearing
down hard with his thumbs and crushing his windpipe.
The killer began thrashing about wildly, trying to cry out
and struggling to free himself, but Will Hardin was too
strong for him. As if knowing that its master had control of
the situation, the big black dog looked on in silence, not
moving a muscle.

Cougar's strong thumbs cut off the air to Lang's windpipe, preventing him even from making a gagging sound.
After a few minutes the killer's face turned purple, and his
body twitched a few times, then went limp. George Lang
was dead.

The young marshal eased him down to the ground under the watchful gaze of the huge dog. After determining
that there was no pulse in the side of Lang's neck, Hardin
hurried to the corner of the toolshed and carefully peeked
around at the house. The back door was open a foot or so,
but the deep shade of the interior kept him from being
able to see anything. He would just have to continue
waiting.

Inside the house, Gordo Silcox placed a chair next to
the partly open door, holding it against the wind, and
made his rounds at the windows. When ten minutes had
elapsed since his cohort had gone to the well, he peered
out the door and looked to see if Lang was returning, but
the only thing moving in the yard was a dust devil.

Pacing back and forth in front of the cookstove, the big
man mumbled to himself, "What's keepin' him? It shouldn't
take but a couple of minutes to fill up that bucket and
bring it back."

Then he remembered that Lang's hat had blown off.
Maybe he was chasing it. Dashing to a window that gave
him a view of the barn, he squinted against the glare of

the sun reflected off the bare ground and focused on a dark object lodged between a tumbleweed and a corral fence post. The dark object was George Lang's hat.

Swearing, Silcox returned to the door and pressed his face past the jamb, then shouted, "George! George!"

There was no reply.

The big killer broke into a cold sweat. He turned toward Veronica, and hope was written on the blonde's face. Pivoting angrily, he stuck his head out the door and called Lang's name again. Still there was no answer—only the wind.

Silcox spun around and glared at Veronica. Pointing a thick finger at her, he bellowed, "If somethin's happened to George, it's *your* fault, woman!"

Meeting his crazed eyes with her steady gaze, she asked incredulously, "*My* fault? I didn't start this devilish venture. You did!"

"You know what I'm talkin' about! I plainly warned you not to tell the Tollivers what was goin' on. If you'd obeyed me, those folks would still be alive, and the three of us would be long gone from here by now! But no! You just had to shoot your mouth off!"

Anger reddened Veronica's lovely face, and giving in to her ire, she screamed at him, "I did not tell either of them one blessed thing! Harriet even asked me if there was something wrong, and I lied to convince her everything was all right. And Martin and I never had a conversation on the matter at all! Don't you dare accuse me of being responsible for their deaths!"

Stomping across the room, Silcox wagged his finger close to her face and roared, "You heard Tolliver right there at that table say that you had told him I wasn't your uncle!"

Veronica was suffused with fury. "You're so dumb! Martin meant that I had unwittingly given the truth away by the fear that was evident on my face! I did my best to hide it, but all the while I was afraid they would figure out that I was your captive, and you would kill them! If you're looking to ascribe blame, look in the mirror!"

Gordo Silcox stood over Veronica, his scruffy face livid with wrath. His voice rising, he exploded, *"You shut up! Just shut up! If I hear any more out of you, I'll beat you to a bloody pulp! And I ain't foolin'! It'd be my pleasure to kill you—and the minute I get rid of your boyfriend, that's exactly what I'm gonna do!"*

Leaning against the corner of the toolshed, Cougar Will Hardin listened to the raised, angry voices coming from the house. Even the wind did not obscure the shouted words. Hardin's muscles tensed. His first impulse upon hearing the threats was to race across the yard and burst through the door. But he restrained himself. Silcox had Veronica in his clutches, and Cougar dared not endanger her further. Though it galled him, he knew he had to be patient, as Red Wolf had taught him.

Abruptly Hardin remembered something else Red Wolf had taught him: Frighten your prey as much as possible, since a hunted creature will make foolish mistakes if it is afraid. Pondering, he wondered what he could do to rattle Silcox and instill fear in him.

Pulling away from the corner of the toolshed, he turned to look at Deputy, and his gaze settled on the corpse of George Lang. The face was somewhat bloated and was now the color of dead ashes—and suddenly the lawman knew what he was going to do.

Working at the window on the back side of the toolshed, Hardin finally jimmied it loose, shoved it open, then climbed inside. At the sight of the bodies of the rancher and his wife, his stomach lurched, and he looked away quickly. Finding what he had hoped to find—a length of rope—he climbed back through the window, stood on the table that held the washbasin, then looped one end of the rope around a jutting rafter. He jumped down from the table and walked over to Lang's body, and while Deputy looked on with his ponderous head cocked, Hardin picked up the corpse and carried it toward the dangling rope.

Inside the house, Gordo Silcox had exhausted his tirade at Veronica Simmons and returned to the door. He again

shouted George Lang's name several times and waited for
an answer, but still there was nothing but the mournful
howl of the wind. Turning from the door, the huge man
muttered to himself, "It's got to be Cougar! What else
could be keepin' George? Ain't no way he could have
fallen into the well."

Watching him carefully, Veronica thought that Silcox's
voice sounded ragged and near hysteria, and his face wore
a glazed expression. The man was clearly frightened, and
he looked as if he were about to split apart.

The buffalo hunter went to each window again, staring
past the fluttering curtains at the sunbaked land, and the
need to know what had happened to Lang rose within him
like a bubble rising through water. Looking over his shoulder as he walked toward the door, he told Veronica, "I've
got to go out there, girlie . . . and you're goin' with me. If
your boyfriend has George, I'll need you for a shield."

Reaching the door, he peered out—and what he saw
made him stiffen. Drawing a shuddering breath, gripping
the door with one hand and the frame with the other, he
stared out as if transfixed and unable to move. The body of
George Lang, with its hideous, pallid, bloated face, was
hanging upside down by the ankles from the rafter of the
toolshed, swaying like a pendulum in the wind.

"What is it?" called Veronica, craning her neck in an
attempt to see past him.

Silcox did not answer. Finally pulling himself together,
he closed the door and stepped back, and when he turned
toward Veronica, his face was devoid of color. He licked
his dry lips with an equally dry tongue and stared at her.

"What is it?" the schoolteacher repeated.

"George is dead. He's hangin' out there like a gutted
deer . . . put there by your boyfriend."

Veronica felt her pulse quicken. Will Hardin had now
eliminated George Lang—which meant that soon her nightmare would be over.

Silcox pulled his gun and opened the door cautiously.
The hot wind whipped him in the face. Taking a deep

breath, he shouted, "Cougar! I have your woman in here! You want her to die?"

He waited for an answer, but none came.

There was just the wind.

Cold sweat ran down Gordo Silcox's face, soaking his unkempt beard and mustache. His shirt was sticking to the center of his back where it, too, was soaked. Pivoting, he turned toward Veronica and growled, "Okay, girlie, you and me are leavin' this place."

Moving to the table, he picked up his greasy hat and clapped it on his head. Then, holstering his gun, he untied Veronica from the chair and lifted her to her feet, but she stumbled slightly, stiff from sitting in one position for so long. Locking her neck in the crook of his left arm, he pulled the gun and forced her toward the door, kicking the chair out of the way and shoving the door wide open with his foot. Then Silcox inched himself and the blonde onto the porch, with the muzzle of his cocked revolver pressed at the base of her skull.

Veronica felt as though she would wretch at the sight of George Lang's corpse swinging in the wind, but she was not sorry the killer was dead. Still, she hurriedly averted her eyes.

Silcox dragged Veronica to the edge of the porch, then halted. Looking warily back and forth, he shouted, "Cougar! I know you're out there! You better listen real careful! This gun is cocked and has a hair trigger, so even if you shoot me, your woman will get a bullet in this pretty head of hers!"

The dry, hot wind whistled around the eaves of the house and toolshed, but there was no response from Will Hardin.

Pain shot through Veronica's knee as the killer pulled her toward his horse, and although the wind tossed her disheveled hair into her eyes, stinging them, her hands were still tied, so she could do nothing to brush it away. Cautiously and methodically, Silcox placed Veronica in the saddle, then climbed up behind her—all the while keep-

ing the gun pointed at her. Reaching around her with his
left hand and taking the reins, he pressed the gun to the
base of her skull again, then shouted, "Cougar! Me and
your woman are leavin'! And I'm warnin' you, if I see so
much as your shadow, she dies!"

Veronica did not know where Will Hardin was hiding,
but one thing she *did* know: His tactics definitely were
working on Silcox. The man was completely shaken. She
was confident that the lawman knew exactly what he was
doing. He had needed Gordo Silcox out in the open, and
now he had him there.

It was nearing noon as they headed out of the Tollivers'
yard, and the killer looked back almost continually as they
rode out. There was still no sign of Cougar Will Hardin—
yet Veronica had the sense that Silcox could almost feel
the dauntless lawman's breath on the back of his neck. It
would all climax soon . . . of that she was sure.

From inside the toolshed Will Hardin watched the buffalo hunter and Veronica ride off, and the desire for vengeance burned in his veins like molten fire. Gordo Silcox
had murdered his family and kidnapped the woman he
loved. The only satisfaction Cougar had now was that his
prey was frightened—and soon Silcox would make a fatal
mistake.

Chapter Thirteen

Gordo Silcox rode hard for two hours. All the while the burning sun sucked moisture from his massive body, and the thirst in his throat grew increasingly intense. Although Veronica Simmons was also suffering, Silcox had no concern for her, only for himself. He had, at least, finally untied her hands—but that was only because he knew there was no way she could escape now. Familiar with that part of the country, Silcox knew he would have to wait till he reached Horseshoe Creek to satisfy his thirst.

He finally allowed his exhausted mount to slow to a walk, but the killer kept a steady watch over his shoulder. The foothills were rolling and uneven, with thick grass in the open areas and countless patches of heavy brush and clumps of trees where a man could easily hide. Squinting, Silcox thought he caught a movement in a clump of trees thirty yards behind.

He swore angrily and straightened in the saddle, again spurring the horse to a gallop. Thirty seconds of hard riding carried them into a stand of wind-whipped trees, and Silcox wheeled the horse around and backed it farther into the shade. He then peered intently toward the spot where he thought he had seen movement.

When Hardin did not materialize, the buffalo hunter

cursed again. He realized that either he had seen something else or his imagination was playing tricks on him, but he had not seen Cougar.

Just then a young buck deer emerged into the sunlight from the spot where Silcox had seen the movement, and the outlaw felt the tension drain from his body. Holstering his gun, he reached into a shirt pocket and pulled out a plug of tobacco, then tore off a chaw with his teeth.

Looking up at him, Veronica remarked, "I would think that stuff would only intensify your thirst."

"Naw," he replied. "It works up some saliva."

"When we come to some water, will you please let me drink?"

"Maybe."

"If I die of dehydration, you won't have me for a shield anymore, you know," she pointed out coolly.

"Drive a hard bargain, don't you?"

"I want to live."

"You'll stand a better chance if your boyfriend leaves us alone."

"Hah!" Veronica countered. "My *only* chance is for him to come."

Silcox merely turned his head and spat a brown stream, then scanned their back trail once more and headed back into the sunlight.

After another half hour Horseshoe Creek came into view, wending its way across the rugged country and resembling a thin silver ribbon as it threaded snakelike through the hills. Eager for a drink, Silcox put the horse into a full gallop. As he sped over the rolling land, he lost sight of the creek directly in front of them as it dipped into a draw for a mile or so.

Suddenly Gordo Silcox's horse stepped into a hole hidden by the long grass and went down, sending its passengers flying. Both Veronica and he slammed the ground hard, then rolled several times before coming to a stop. The killer quickly picked himself up, swearing and placing his hat on his head. The horse was also back on its feet, but it was limping about and whinnying.

The buffalo hunter strode over to where Veronica lay, holding her knee and gritting her teeth in pain. Looking down at her with a smirk on his face, he snickered, "Guess your boyfriend ain't too close, girlie. If he was, he'd have jumped me for sure when we took that spill." He looked back, then muttered, " 'Course, there weren't no way of knowing we was goin' to fall. If he's followin', he's probably too far away to do somethin'—and I ain't gonna let him get no closer."

Bending, Silcox grabbed Veronica's wrist and yanked her to her feet. "C'mon," he growled, "back in the saddle."

The horse nickered, holding its right foreleg off the ground. Silcox cursed, released the young woman's wrist, and hurried to the horse. Kneeling, he held the animal's foreleg and examined it thoroughly, then swore again. He turned to the blonde and said, "His leg's hurt purty bad. Ain't broke, but I think it's sprained. C'mon, let's walk to the creek. We'll give him a few minutes' rest."

Leading the horse, Silcox kept Veronica alongside him. He took another look over his shoulder. There was no sign of Cougar, but the needles that pricked his spine from top to bottom told him the man was out there somewhere.

Veronica began to lag behind. Halting, Silcox blared, "Hey, keep up, will you?"

"Haven't you an ounce of compassion?" Veronica countered angrily. "That fall hurt my knee some more. And you're dragging that poor animal too fast, as well. Can't you see he's hurting?"

"Yeah, two limpin' critters on my hands!" spat Silcox. He coldly regarded the horse, muttering, "I oughtta shoot him since I won't be able to ride him no more." Glaring at her, he added, "Oughtta shoot you, too."

"You're worried because Will is on our trail and it won't be easy to stay ahead of him now."

"Shut your trap!" bawled the huge man. "We'll get some water in our bodies, and then I'll think of somethin'."

Pushing on, they topped the rise that overlooked the creek, with Silcox reaching the spot a pace ahead of Veronica. He looked out on the shallow valley spread out below, then suddenly threw out a hand to stop the young woman from heading down the hill. Kneeling on the creek bank at the bottom of the hill some forty yards below was a lone Cheyenne brave, filling several canteens with water. His back was toward them, and he was unaware of their presence. Silcox eyed the Indian's husky pinto and suddenly smiled. All he had to do was kill the Indian, and they would have a horse to ride.

Pulling Veronica and the injured horse back from the crest, Silcox sighed with relief. If they had ridden over the top, the Indian would have heard the hoofbeats.

Veronica looked wide-eyed at the big man and whispered, "What are you going to do?"

"I'm gonna get us an able-bodied mount—that pinto," he said drily.

"You're going to kill the Indian?" she asked, horrified.

"That's right."

"What if there are more of them around?"

"Girlie, my eyes have been peeled every minute. There ain't nobody around." Then looking behind them, he added, "Except for your lover boy. He's lurkin' somewhere on our trail. I can feel him in my bones. I gotta hurry and kill the Indian so's we can stay ahead of Cougar."

As he spoke he half-carried her over to his horse. "I can't take no chance of you tryin' to escape while I'm killin' that redskin, so I'm gonna tie you to the saddle. I know my horse ain't goin' nowhere—not with *his* sprained leg."

"Mr. Silcox, listen," Veronica countered, her voice quivering, "that Indian isn't alone. If you kill him, there will be others to reckon with. They'll torture us and kill us."

Shaking his head, Silcox retorted, "I got good eyes, and I say he's alone."

"Didn't you see what he was doing?" she asked. "He was filling canteens—a number of them. Be sensible! Do you think he's going to drink all that water by himself?"

"I dunno," mumbled Silcox, hoisting Veronica into the saddle. "Maybe he's takin' off on a long journey." Pulling a short length of slender rope from a saddlebag, he added with a chuckle, "In fact, I *know* he's takin' off on a long journey. To the Happy Hunting Ground!"

"You fool!" she breathed, keeping her voice low. "Do you know what Cheyenne do to a white man who kills one of their own? Especially from stealth?"

"Hey, you're sittin' up high, girlie," the buffalo hunter quipped while lashing her wrists to the saddle horn. "Look around. See any other redskins?" He grinned. "Don't even bother answerin'. The only thing that matters is stayin' ahead of Will Hardin—and a lame horse is no better'n a dead horse. That redskin at the creek has what I need, so it's a plain and simple matter: Kill the no-good redskin and take his pinto."

Veronica winced as the big man jerked the knot tight on her wrists. As an added measure of precaution, Silcox pulled his filthy bandanna from his pocket and tied it around the young woman's mouth, gagging her. "There! Now you can't do nothin' stupid—like holler out to that redskin."

A half mile from where young Spotted Fox was filling stolen Army canteens, resting in a stand of trees on a high hill overlooking the valley, were Black Shirt, the leader of the renegade Cheyenne band, and nineteen men. Just over three years had passed since Black Shirt had led the band of braves in revolt against the white man's law and jumped the Wind River Indian Reservation in north-central Wyoming, where some of the Cheyenne had been placed along with the Shoshone nation.

Like the young brave at the creek, all the renegades were clad only in loincloths and wore headbands with single feathers—except for their leader. He wore a full headdress he had stolen from his father, a Cheyenne chief, and a threadbare black shirt that he had taken from a trapper he had killed two years previously. It was then that the warrior had forsaken his given name and dubbed himself Black Shirt.

The renegade leader was sitting cross-legged on the ground, enjoying the cool of the shade and the wind that whistled through the trees. Suddenly a brave named Standing Elk came dashing up to him, saying excitedly, "Black Shirt! We may have trouble! Something suspicious is happening on the far hill."

Looking up at the brave, Black Shirt's brow furrowed as he asked, "What do you mean?"

"Come see!" replied Standing Elk, motioning Black Shirt to follow him.

Seconds later the entire band stood in the shadows at the edge of the trees and looked across the valley, watching as Gordo Silcox tied and gagged Veronica Simmons on the horse.

"What do you think the white man is doing, Black Shirt?" Standing Elk asked.

Shrugging, Black Shirt said, "What whites do to each other is not my concern. They—"

He stopped short as the huge buffalo hunter yanked his rifle from the saddle boot and in a half crouch hurried toward the crest of the hill, levering a cartridge into the chamber. Reaching the crest, the killer peered down at Spotted Fox, who was still kneeling on the creek bank, filling canteens, his copper-colored skin shining in the brilliant sunlight. He was as unaware of the white man watching him as he was of his fellow Cheyenne.

The wind plucked at Silcox's wide hat brim as he braced his feet and shouldered the rifle. Black Shirt was about to call out a warning to his brave when the giant squeezed the trigger, the rifle boomed, and a black hole appeared between Spotted Fox's shoulders. The young Indian stiffened, bowing his shoulders against the slug's impact, then toppled facedown into the stream. His torso was still on the bank, but his head and shoulders were submerged in the swift-moving water.

While Gordo Silcox waved the rifle over his head and

emitted a wild, triumphant yell as he bounded down the slope toward the stream, the renegade Indians gasped in horror. Over the report of the rifle that echoed across the valley, Black Shirt cursed the white man. As he and his braves dashed back amid the trees for their horses, the renegade leader swore by his gods that he would avenge Spotted Fox's death.

Hearing the rifle shot, then Silcox's fiendish laugh, Veronica Simmons closed her eyes, falling forward onto her lashed hands. *Oh, God,* she prayed, *let this awful torment end.* She shook her head slowly, dreading what was going to happen to her if the dead brave had companions somewhere nearby.

Dear God, the young woman thought, her eyes still closed, *why do there have to be men like Silcox in this world? Why—*

"Ronnie!" came a half-whispered voice from beside her.

At first the harried blonde thought her mind was playing tricks on her. Then she realized it was not her imagination. Jerking her head up, she looked down from the horse's back into the face of the man she loved. She tried muttering his name despite the gag, then burst into tears.

"I didn't want to frighten you," he said softly, smiling lovingly as he untied the filthy bandanna, throwing it on the ground.

Veronica's dirt-streaked face showed a combination of joy and relief. "Oh, Will!" she breathed, her voice breaking into sobs, "I thought you'd never come!"

Rage burned through Will Hardin like wind-driven fire when he saw the bruises on Veronica's face and neck. He wanted to first crush and maim, then kill Gordo Silcox, whose gleeful splashing and childish laughter carried up over the crest of the grassy slope.

Laying his rifle down, Cougar began untying the rope that bound Veronica to the saddle horn. Her hands were blue, for the rope had been tied so tight, it had cut off the circulation. As he worked at getting the knot loose, he commented, "I was staying in the low spots as I followed you, but I saw Silcox walking toward the creek with the rifle in his hand, and then I heard the shot. Did he kill something?"

"Some*one*," Veronica replied. "A Cheyenne brave." She explained about Silcox's horse getting injured and the buffalo hunter's plan to murder the Indian and steal his pinto. "Will," she said fearfully, "we've got to get out of here! There are undoubtedly other Cheyenne close by!"

The knot finally loosened some. Hurrying to release her, Hardin observed, "You're probably right. As soon as I get you free, I'll go after Silcox. My horse is stashed in a gully about fifty yards back. Run down there and stay till I come back."

Veronica shook her head and explained, "I . . . I can't run, Will. I've got a badly sprained knee. As a matter of fact, at this point I can barely walk. I'm afraid that if you want to get me to safety quickly, you'll have to carry me."

The rope fell loose from her wrists, and Hardin swept Veronica out of the saddle, cradling her in his arms. She hugged his neck tightly as he started running back toward his horse.

Suddenly Silcox's splashing and laughter ceased, and the lawman half-turned back toward the creek. "Sounds like he's about ready to return," Cougar told Veronica softly. "There isn't time to take you to the gully." He looked over his shoulder, adding, "There's a big rock back there. I'll set you down behind it."

Hardin pivoted, and Veronica gasped loudly. Standing in front of them was the huge black dog, its tongue hanging from its mouth as it sat looking at them. "Don't worry, Ronnie," Cougar assured her as he dashed toward the large rock that jutted out of the sod some fifty feet away. "That's my new deputy. He's on our side."

"Your new deputy?"

"Yes. The town made me marshal after Zack Traynor's death. It's a long story, but I found the dog in the mountains when I started tracking you, and we took a liking to

each other. Fortunately. 'Cause it turns out he's tougher
than old harness leather, plus he saved my life. When I
decided to keep him, I named him Deputy."

The animal stayed on Cougar's heels, and as they reached
the rock and the lawman started to place Veronica behind
it, she suggested, "I know I'll be more exposed, but I
think my leg will hurt a lot less if I sit on the rock and let
my leg hang."

Hardin gently sat her on the boulder, then told the dog,
"Deputy, this is Ronnie. She's real special to me, so you
stay here and take care of her." Veronica eyed the huge
dog warily, but Cougar assured her, "It's okay. He'll do as
I say. You're safe with him beside you."

With that, Hardin levered a cartridge into his rifle's
chamber and ran hard back toward the creek.

Deputy whined, took a few steps toward Cougar, then
halted, staring at his master. He moved close to Veronica,
who cautiously patted the dog's big head, saying, "You
know Will's in danger, don't you, boy? And you don't
know whether to obey him and stay with me, or to disobey and go join him, right?"

Deputy whined again and looked into the woman's eyes,
then back to his master. He started forward once more,
then stopped, obeying the command he had been given.
Facing forward, as unmoving as the boulder he sat beside,
the dog watched and listened and waited.

Nearing the crest of the slope, Will Hardin removed
his hat and slid down on his belly, and then he crept
forward until he could see over the edge. Gordo Silcox,
his rifle lying on the bank beside him, was taking the
knife off the dead Indian's waist. Hardin got to his knees.
It was time to act.

The buffalo hunter slipped the Indian's knife under his
belt, then stood and stepped to the pinto, standing on the
far side of the animal and checking the bridle. He was
about to turn and reach for his rifle when he abruptly
started, gasping. Standing halfway down the slope, hold-

ing his own rifle at waist level with both hands, was the formidable figure of Marshal Will Hardin. The ominous black muzzle of the repeater rifle was pointing straight at the killer's broad chest, just over the top of the pinto's back.

Cougar's harsh voice cut the air like a bullwhip. "Don't bother going for your weapon, Silcox! Raise your hands and step around the horse!"

Instead of complying, a broad grin worked its way across the ugly man's bearded face, and a glint appeared in his piglike eyes. Meeting Cougar's icy gray glare, he laughed malevolently and retorted, "Reckon it had to come to this, didn't it? We finally get our showdown after a long chase."

Despite his inner fury, Hardin's reply was cold. "Yeah. Finally." The wind plucked at his hair as he paused for a few seconds, then stated flatly, "You've got a choice: Die right now—or live long enough to ride back to Sheridan where you can take the plunge at the end of a rope."

Cougar felt the tension between them as Silcox stared at him with a hard, unrelenting gaze, then spoke in a flat and emotionless voice. "I'm not really fond of the choice you're givin' me, lawman."

Hardin countered blandly, "I don't really care how you feel about it. I told you to get your hands up and step around the horse. Now do it."

The bearded killer gently slapped the pinto's rump with his free hand, and the animal walked away, exposing the revolver in Silcox's hand. It was cocked and the black bore was dead centered on Will Hardin's chest. "Nice of that there pony to hide my hands from you, wasn't it?" the giant mocked. "Made it right easy to get this here revolver out of my holster."

Hardin tensed as a devilish smirk worked its way across Silcox's ugly mouth.

The killer continued, "You can squeeze the trigger on that rifle and no doubt put your bullet through my heart, Cougar. But a bullet-struck man just might have some reflex. Fire that weapon, and you stand a good chance of takin' my slug in your own chest."

"That can work the other way, too," warned the marshal. "You shoot me, and there's a .44 slug just itching to see if your heart is really made out of stone."

Still grinning evilly, Silcox chuckled, "Well, now, Hardin. I'd say it looks like we've got us another old-fashioned standoff here."

Sudden movement on the top of the hill made Silcox lift his eyes. Deputy, his hackles raised, was standing and staring down at the buffalo hunter. The huge black dog was outlined against the sky like an apparition, and the menacing beast's upper lip was curled, exposing its razor-sharp fangs. The grin faded on Silcox's face as a deep growl began to build in Deputy's throat.

His eyes round with fright, Silcox looked back at the marshal and declared, "I know you can hear real well, which means you can hear that growlin', so you know I ain't lyin' when I tell you there's a huge dog lookin' down on us, ready to spring. We'd better use these guns to kill that monster!"

Not turning around to look at the dog, Hardin scoffed, "Why would I want to do that? He's *my* dog—and he's growling at *you*."

Gordo Silcox stared for a long moment at the marshal, then ran his nervous gaze back to the growling dog. "You ain't takin' me, Cougar!" he abruptly shouted, looking at the lawman again. "You ain't takin' me to no gallows!"

The growl increased in volume as Deputy slowly walked down the hill.

Hardin snapped, "Ease the hammer down on your gun and let it drop, Silcox!"

Holding the gun steady, the killer countered, "No! Call off your mutt, or I'll shoot you, and then I'll shoot him!"

"Pull your trigger and my dog will tear out your throat before you get a shot at him!" Cougar warned. "And you won't be the first killer he's chewed into little pieces."

Silcox again shifted his wary gaze to Deputy, who was

now standing a few feet away. When their eyes met, the huge dog snapped its jaws repeatedly, snarling ferociously. Its dark eyes glued to the killer, it stood poised and ready to spring, saliva dripping from its mouth.

"He's waiting for one of two things, Silcox," Hardin remarked calmly. "Word from me to jump you . . . or for you to make a move. If you're thinking of trying to kill him first, I'll blow a hole in your chest before you can swing your gun on him. The standoff is over—'cause either I'll get you or my dog will . . . but one of us *will* get you. And either way, you're dead!"

Gordo Silcox hesitated, and Will Hardin could almost feel the turnings of the man's mind as he debated what to do: Could he somehow get out of this seemingly impossible situation—or not? If he let go of the gun and surrendered, he would hang for sure.

Cougar finally rasped, "I know what you're thinking, Silcox, but drop the gun! At least you'll live long enough to hang. And who knows? It may be weeks before the circuit judge comes around to try you. But if you try to shoot your way out, you'll die now!"

Thinking about his choices, Gordo Silcox suddenly got a picture of himself plunging through the trapdoor of a gallows, a rope around his neck. It was enough to make his blood run cold—and to make his decision. He would take his chances here and now, because nobody took a drop at the end of a rope and walked away. At least here he had a chance, slim though it was. And slim was better than none. He already had his gun trained on Cougar, so he would shoot the lawman first, then turn the gun on the dog as it came at him. Hopefully when Hardin reflexively fired when *he* was shot, the slug would go wild. Holding his breath so as to steady himself, Silcox thought, *You're about to die, Cougar! Now!*

Deputy sensed the killer's move before he made it, and like an ebony streak the dog was on the man. Silcox's gun discharged, but his aim was spoiled as the animal's powerful jaws clamped down on his gun arm.

Silcox screamed, trying to pull free of the snarling dog, but Deputy clung tenaciously to him, tearing shirt and flesh as he savagely gnashed the arm. The buffalo hunter went down on the bank of the creek, and his revolver sailed into the water. Silcox pounded the beast with his left fist as hard as he could, but the effort served only to intensify Deputy's fury, and he shook his head angrily, ripping Silcox's arm even more.

Clenching his teeth, the terrified killer squeezed his eyes shut, and the agony he was experiencing came out as an ear-splitting scream as he writhed on the creek bank. "Cougar-r-r!" Silcox wailed. "Get him off me-e-e!"

As Will Hardin walked casually down the slope, he was unaware that Veronica Simmons had left the rock and limped back to the crest, where she watched the scene taking place below her with an expression of horror and satisfaction.

Reaching the creek bank, Hardin stood with his arms crossed over his chest a few feet away from where Deputy was exacting justice. Silcox opened his eyes, and when he saw Hardin glaring down at him, he screeched, "Please, I'm beggin' you, Cougar! Get him off me!"

As the lawman pictured the three graves that now lay behind the cabin in the Bighorn Mountains, he remembered those final moments he had had with his father, and Obadiah Hardin's last words: *"Get 'em, son. Make 'em pay."* Fire filled the young marshal's veins once more. "The rest of them have already paid, Pa," he said softly. "And this filthy buzzard is going to pay, too. I'll see that he stretches a rope—but first he's going to feel my personal vengeance."

"Deputy, stop!" Hardin abruptly commanded.

The slavering dog immediately let go of Silcox's bleeding arm and looked up at its master. "Come here, boy," Hardin ordered, and Deputy responded immediately.

Silcox lay on his back and grabbed his wounded arm with his other hand, looking at the damage. His shirtsleeve was in tatters, soaked with the blood that poured from numerous punctures and gashes.

Will Hardin patted his dog's head, saying, "You disobeyed me and left Ronnie, but it's okay. Looks like I owe you again, big fella!"

Just then the young marshal caught sight of Veronica standing at the top of the rise above him. Hardin gave her a reassuring look, and she smiled. Ruffling Deputy's thick coat, he pointed up the slope and told the dog, "Go stay with Ronnie, boy."

Instantly the dog bounded up the hill, then sat beside the blonde and looked down at its master.

Cougar turned back to Silcox, who was staring up at him with hate-filled eyes, and for a long moment the heavy silence between them was almost palpable. Then Hardin said through clenched teeth, "You're going to hang, mister, but right now I've got a score to settle with you."

Leaning over, the marshal removed the Indian's knife from under Silcox's belt with one hand while jerking the killer's other knife from its sheath. He tossed them onto the far bank of the creek, then began unbuckling his own gun belt.

Gordo Silcox staggered to his feet, a glint of hope showing in his piglike eyes. Eyeing Hardin, the killer spat and grinned in anticipation of the bare-handed brawl about to take place between the two enemies.

Will Hardin tossed his gun belt, along with his sheathed knife, toward Veronica, and they landed just short of the crest. The blonde limped down, picked them up, and sat down on the grassy slope. Deputy followed closely and snuggled beside her.

Leering wickedly at the smaller man, Gordo Silcox grunted, "You're gonna be sorry you did this, Cougar. One arm's torn up, but I'm a whole lot bigger than you, and I can still whip you. I'm gonna drown you in the creek, then take your woman with me."

Cougar flicked a glance up the hill, then chuckled. "You going to take my dog as well?"

Silcox ran his dark gaze to Deputy, then swallowed hard, not commenting.

Hardin moved close, opening and closing his fists. "You killed my family," he breathed hotly. "You kidnapped Ronnie and brutalized her. Your final retribution will come when you hang . . . but right now I'm going to have my pound of flesh."

"You ain't big enough to get a pound of flesh from me, little man," retorted Silcox, charging toward the sinewy lawman.

Cougar set himself and lashed out with a vicious blow that caught the huge man on the jaw, and the marshal felt the impact of it all the way to his ankles. The blow sent Silcox reeling backward, and he tripped over the body of the Indian and toppled into the water. Hardin swooped down on him like a hungry carnivorous bird. Their bodies smacked the water hard, and they went under the surface, hitting bottom four feet down.

Both men came up, fists swinging. Silcox landed a meaty fist on Hardin's temple and knocked him flat in the creek. As he closed in to do more damage, Cougar rolled underneath the surface, tripping the giant. Silcox went down with his mouth open, drawing water into his lungs. Rising, he broke the surface gagging and coughing.

Watching the combatants intently, Veronica sank her fingers into Deputy's coat, pulling for the man she loved. Suddenly movement caught her eye to her right, and turning her head, she saw a band of Cheyenne galloping up. She felt her blood run cold.

The dog went rigid and stood up, growling. Terrified, Veronica's voice was unsteady and her body trembled as she gripped the dog and whispered, "No, boy! You stay here with me!" Deputy stood stiffly, eyeing the Cheyenne and growling continuously.

Black Shirt led his braves to a halt on the crest ten yards from where Veronica sat. The renegade leader regarded her for a moment, then dismounted, and his braves then slipped from their horses as well.

Veronica's heart leapt to her throat, and breathing became a chore. But instead of heading toward her, the Cheyenne leader focused on the two men whaling savagely at each other, then started down the slope, levering a cartridge into the repeater rifle he carried in his hands. The other braves cocked the hammers of their single-shot rifles and followed Black Shirt toward the creek.

Veronica felt her terror down to her bones. Her blue eyes huge with fright, she tried to scream a warning to Hardin, but the sound locked in her throat.

Chapter Fourteen

As Will Hardin and Gordo Silcox clashed on the bank of Horseshoe Creek, the lawman was the first of the combatants to catch sight of the Indians. After driving a solid blow to Gordo Silcox's jaw, dropping the giant to his knees in the water, he sensed movement from the slope and glanced up. Coming toward the two men was a band of Cheyenne, while on the crest, sitting as still as statues, were Veronica Simmons and Deputy.

Cougar was about to determine whether Veronica was all right when he saw Silcox lunging for his rifle on the creek bank. The lawman quickly waded out after him, prepared to kick the weapon from his enemy's hand, but the buffalo hunter saw the Indians and paused, his hand inches from the rifle. The Cheyenne wearing the black shirt eyed the killer and shook his head in warning.

Silcox was still focused on the renegades, his face pale with fear, when Cougar sank his powerful fingers into his foe's buffalo-hide vest and pulled him back into the stream. Grabbing the man's enormous head, Hardin shoved it under the surface, but Silcox struggled until his brute force enabled him to best his opponent, and he splashed up through the water, lifting Hardin off his feet.

The men continued to trade violent blows, and the young marshal wondered why the Cheyenne had not

stopped the brutal fight—and what was going to happen
when it was over. He glanced away from his adversary just
long enough to look at the leader's face, and it was clear
from Black Shirt's expression that he was enjoying the
battle.

Driven by revenge, Will Hardin's strength was even
greater than it usually was. He planted his feet and drove
a powerful blow to Gordo Silcox's stomach, and the giant
went down on the bank, sucking hard for air, his strength
beginning to wane.

Hardin stood knee-deep in the water, his muscular chest
heaving, and growled, "Get up, Silcox! I'm not finished
with you yet!"

Drawing on his reserves, the killer scrambled to his feet
and roared, "I'm gonna crush you to pieces, Har—"

The giant's word was cut off by a rock-hard fist smashing
his mouth. Blood rushed over his teeth as he staggered
back from the blow. Then Cougar slammed the big man
hard on the nose with one fist and cracked his jaw with the
other, and blood trickled from both his nose and mouth.

Again Cougar glanced at the renegades, finding that
Black Shirt was smiling at his companions, obviously pleased
that the giant was being bested by the smaller man.

Pulling back his muscular right arm, Will Hardin deliv-
ered a violent punch to Gordo Silcox's jaw, and Silcox's
feet left the rocky bottom of the creek. He smacked the
water, then sank.

Breathing hard, Cougar bent over and hoisted his foe's
enormous body out of the water. The man was conscious
but glassy-eyed, with no more strength left in him. Hardin
dragged him onto the bank and held him up, and Silcox's
massive arms hung limply at his sides. The lawman's eyes
were still filled with vengeance as he held the giant erect
with his left hand, then cocked his right arm and hissed,
"I've got one last reminder for what you did to my father,
my mother, and my grandfather!"

The final blow had all the force of a mule's kick,
pounding Silcox into unconsciousness. Opening his hand,

Will Hardin let the huge body fall to the ground with a thud.

Hardin stood over his adversary, gasping for air. He looked up at Veronica, who was still seated as though made of stone, her eyes darting back and forth between Cougar and the Indians. Turning toward the black-shirted leader, the lawman eyed him warily as the Cheyenne stepped up to him.

To his surprise, the Indian half smiled, then said, "I am Black Shirt. My braves and I want to congratulate you on the way you handled a man so much larger than yourself."

"Thanks," Hardin breathed. "But what now?"

Black Shirt arched his eyebrows and replied, "You are expecting me to harm you. I see it in your eyes."

The lawman smiled wryly. "How could I not? Everyone in Wyoming knows how Black Shirt feels about whites." His face grew serious, and he gestured at the dead brave being placed on his pinto by his fellow Cheyenne. "I am sorry that your friend had to die the way he did."

The Indian nodded and looked down at Silcox. "Wake him up," he commanded Hardin, his voice suddenly ice-cold.

Cougar repeatedly dipped Silcox's head in the stream until he came to. Stretching him out on the bank, he stood over him and ordered, "Get up, Silcox. Black Shirt wants to talk to you."

As Gordo Silcox's head cleared and he got to his feet, he looked from Will Hardin's face to Black Shirt's, and his own face blanched with fear. "You . . . you're Black Shirt?" he stammered.

The Cheyenne regarded him with fiery eyes and blurted, "You shot Spotted Fox in the back!"

Wiping blood from his swollen lips, the giant raised his hands in protest and declared, "Not me, Black Shirt! It was him! He may be wearin' a badge, but he's a killer! Hardin's the one who shot your brave!"

Cougar shook his head and started to speak when the renegade leader spat at Silcox, "You lie! My braves and I

saw you do it after you bound the woman with yellow hair
to the saddle of your horse! For killing a Cheyenne brave,
you will learn Cheyenne justice!"

Gordo Silcox's puffy eyes bulged. In a frenzy of horror
he screeched, "Cougar! Don't let 'em take me! I'll take the
rope! Don't let 'em have me! They'll torture me! I'll die a
slow, agonizin' death! Cougar, please!"

The Cheyenne leader's black eyes flashed. Pointing his
rifle at Silcox, he snapped, "You will be quiet!" Turning to
Hardin, his face was solemn as he announced, "If you do
not try to interfere with our taking of this murderer, you
and the woman will live. Otherwise, you will both die."

Silcox screamed again, "No! Hardin, you can't leave me!
Have mercy, I beg you!"

Cougar shot an icy glance at the killer, then explained
to the Indian leader, "I am Marshal Will Hardin of Sheridan. This man murdered my parents and my grandfather
in cold blood, then kidnapped and beat my woman. I want
to take him back to Sheridan to be tried and hung. Surely
you can understand that."

The renegade leader shook his head slowly. "He will
receive Cheyenne punishment. I repeat: If you try to stop
us from taking him, Marshal Hardin, you and your woman
will die. Further argument will exhaust my patience."

Will Hardin glanced at the braves ringing them, watching him carefully. He knew Black Shirt meant business,
leaving him no choice. Though he was disappointed that
he would be deprived of seeing Silcox hang, he knew that
justice would be carried out on him by the Cheyenne. He
threw Silcox a cold stare, nodded his silent assent to Black
Shirt, then turned away without a word. Bending down,
he retrieved his rifle, then started up the hill toward
Veronica. As Cougar climbed the slope, Silcox screamed
at him, begging for help, but the lawman did not look
back.

Four strong braves grasped the buffalo hunter, who
kicked and flailed, his cries echoing off the hillside. With a
sudden burst of strength he threw off his captors and

bolted after the marshal, shrieking, "Cougar-r-r!" But he got only a few steps before he was tackled and dragged back and his hands quickly bound behind him.

Silcox's cries could still be heard as Marshal Will Hardin reached Veronica Simmons. She was standing now, holding his hat, knife, and gun belt. The lawman smiled at her, then took his things and put them on. Deputy suddenly jumped up on his master, putting his huge paws on the wiry lawman's chest and almost knocking him over. Cougar laughed as he patted the animal's head, saying, "You're a good dog, Deputy. A very good dog."

Removing the dog's paws, Cougar stepped directly in front of Veronica. They looked into each other's eyes for a moment, then reached for each other and held each other tightly. They stood locked in an embrace as the Indians rode away with Gordo Silcox, whose screams of terror slowly faded away. When the terrible sound had finally died out, Hardin leaned back and looked into Veronica's eyes, asking softly, "Are you all right?"

Nodding, she replied, "I'm fine now, Will, but I need to know something, and it can't wait."

"Yes?"

"When . . . when those killers were taking me away from the Welton place, you called out that you love me. Did you mean as a friend, or—"

Touching her face gently, he answered, "I meant it the way it sounded. Veronica Simmons, I am in love with you. Head over heels in love with you." He smiled. "Does that answer your question."

Tears brimmed Veronica's eyes. "Oh, yes!" Then she cocked her head slightly, adding, "You told Black Shirt that I'm your woman. Did you really mean that?"

"With all my heart. That is, if you want to be."

"Oh, Will!" she exclaimed. "Yes, I want to be! It has been my fondest dream since the day we first met!"

Holding her face in his hands and wiping away her tears with his thumbs, the lawman admitted, "I've probably been in love with you almost as long—it just took me a lot longer to realize it." He sighed and looked into the distance. "I wish it hadn't taken such an awful ordeal for me to figure out just how deeply I love you."

Their lips met, and they enjoyed their first kiss. When they finally parted, Will Hardin swept up the woman he loved in his arms and headed for his horse. As they moved along with Deputy at Hardin's heels, Veronica held tightly to his neck and said, "By the way, I love your adorable dog, too. Almost as much as I love his master."

"Adorable?" Will scoffed. "He's as ugly as they come!" His voice grew serious. "And by the way, I'm glad you made him disobey my orders to stay with you."

"What do you mean?" she asked innocently.

Laughing, he said, "You know darn well what I mean. If you hadn't told him to help me, I might not be carrying you at this very moment."

Reaching the gully, Cougar lifted her into his saddle. He gave her his canteen and let her take a long drink, then hung it back on the saddle horn. Gazing into her blue eyes, he said, "I have no family now, Ronnie. Will you be my family? I mean, by marriage?"

Leaning from the saddle, the beautiful blonde cupped Will Hardin's handsome, scarred face in her hands and asked, "Is this a proposal, Marshal?"

"Yep!" he replied with conviction.

"Then I accept!" she said, and kissed him soundly.

The huge black dog whined, and Cougar rubbed Deputy's furry chest and chuckled. "I won't kiss you, big fella, but don't worry. You're part of the family, too!"

Cougar swung onto his horse behind the beautiful blonde, closing her into his arms as he took the reins. Looking down at the huge black dog, Marshal Will Hardin grinned and ordered, "Okay, Deputy. Let's take Ronnie home!"

THE BADGE: BOOK 19
THE GUNHAWK
by Bill Reno

While tracking a cold-blooded killer, bounty hunter Roy Dennis reluctantly returns to his hometown of Zamora, Kansas, after a thirteen-year absence. As a youth he was forced to become a gunfighter following the murder of his parents—a murder Zamora's citizens did nothing to prevent. When the townspeople, not wanting a gunhawk in their midst, told Roy to leave, he grew bitter toward them. Now a drought has forced the entire town to move to California, but the man hired to be wagonmaster has backed out. Though still feeling resentment toward the town, Roy accepts the job at the urging of his brother-in-law, Marshal Hal Tracy. Roy also knows the journey will give him the chance to get to know Sharon Brett, daughter of Zamora's leading citizen.

The travelers face more than the usual hardships. In an alliance forged out of vindictiveness, escaped murderers Johnny Gregory and Marty Keegan, vowing to kill the gunhawk and the marshal, wreak havoc on the wagon train. Learning of Roy's feelings for Sharon, Keegan plans the ultimate reprisal: He convinces a band of Arapaho to threaten the travelers with massacre if the beautiful Sharon is not given to them. After a fiery attack, it appears that the killer's scheme will succeed.

To the gunhawk falls the job of saving the people who once scorned him—as well as the woman he has come to love.